1984 Arrives in America

George A. Mathewson

VANTAGE PRESS
New York

This is a work of fiction. Any similarity between the names and characters in this book and any real persons, living or dead, is purely coincidental.

FIRST EDITION

Published by Vantage Press, Inc.
419 Park Ave. South, New York, NY 10016

Manufactured in the United States of America
ISBN: 0-533-15249-6

Library of Congress Catalog Card No.: 2005904674

0 9 8 7 6 5 4 3 2 1

To my wife, Ann

Prologue

No one wants to impede our war against terrorism. But questions remain as to how that war is being fought, or should be fought. Since an iron cloak of secrecy has fallen over the operation of our government in the area of national security and the war against terrorism, nobody really knows the actual facts.

In this piece of historical fiction, set around the time of the beginning of the millennium, we get a chance to visualize how the war against terrorism was being fought at that time. This fictional account dramatizes how two actual federal statutes or laws might have been applied at that time. The FISA statute, which stands for the Foreign Intelligence Surveillance Act, and the Patriot Act actually exist. FISA was enacted in 1978 to combat latent terrorism. The Patriot Act was enacted in 2001. They are real life, as are the federal court case decisions interpreting those statutes mentioned in the novel. The federal wire-tapping statute actually exists. And the references to Daniel Ellsberg and Daniel Schorr, two prominent persons in the civil liberties area in the 1970s are also, of course, references to real people. The rest is fiction. If any fictional characters in this novel have any similarity to living persons, that similarity is purely coincidental, unintended, and accidental. This novel does not intend to make the point that its characters actually exist, only that the laws existing in this country at that time were such that the characters might have existed.

FISA created not only new federal rights to conduct surveillance on suspected persons, but also created a new federal court, generally referred to as "the Secret Court." It also created new rules of procedures for cases passing through the court. These rules eliminated the right of opposing parties, or targets, to appear before it, or to be notified of any proceedings against them. In 2001, the Patriot Act then amended FISA to allow many new types of cases to go before the "Secret Court" and to be subjected to the FISA rules. Included in these new cases were those where the primary purpose of the investigation was to initiate an ordinary criminal investigation, cases where the target was being investigated partially because of statements made, which were protected by the First Amendment, and even cases where the defendant was not suspected of committing any crime.

This novel attempts to dramatize how these statutes might have affected journalists, newspapers, government employees, and politicians dealing with sensitive matters in Washington, D.C. at that time.

I

First Impressions—An Enigma

It was Karl Erskine's first day as a G-12, a rating that he had worked nine years to obtain after graduating from George Washington University, and then getting a job with the government. Yet he was stunned as he was led through the doorway of his new office in the "Audio-Visual Unit" of the Foreign Counter-Intelligence Department. The name "Audio-Visual" was apparently an anachronism left over from earlier times at the Department, but the sign inside the door was altogether modern. It stated emphatically:

> HIGH SECURITY AREA: TOP SECRET.
> Security clearance is required before entering this room. Divulging any information about the work done in this room is a felony, punishable by life imprisonment, or a fine of one million dollars, or death.

He had seen some very stiff warnings in his nine years with the U.S. government, but none as threatening as this one. What was going on here? Why the intense concern?

As he looked around the Audio-Visual Unit, he saw a moderate-sized room of maybe 850 square feet, filled with flat desks with computers on them. The computer keyboards, perhaps twelve of them in all, had ordinary monitors behind them, with standard CPUs on the floor next to them. Nothing unusual, really. There were also ten or twelve youngish-looking men and women, along with two or three older employees, perhaps in their forties, who appeared to be supervisors by their badges and manner of sitting at their desk, fidgeting with their computers. Occasionally someone would lean over and chat with the person next to them, but for the most part they seemed to be all business. No joking or laughing; these people were far too serious for anything like that.

As his boss, Roger Kaiser, led Karl through the door, he turned toward Karl and said, “Don’t get freaked out by all these signs, Karl. Just can’t be too careful these days with all those terrorists out there. You never know what they’ll come up with next.” Kaiser then paused for a moment, as if to gather his thoughts a bit, and then continued with his explanation to his new recruit, “This is just a look-see today at your new assignment at the agency. You’ve been selected for this new work based on your progress here at the agency so far, your aptitude scores, and your allegiance to your country. Yes, good old-fashioned patriotism still counts here! Now we’re just going to show you around today, so you can get the lay of the land here, and then give you a chance to ask any questions that you might have about your new assignment.” Nervously, he then added, “That way we can address any concerns you might have about your new assignment. How does that sound to you?”

Karl thought for a second, trying to grasp where the conversation and the new job were going, and then replied, “Fine.” Then after surveying the room for a moment he added, “Since this place looks just like a lot of other rooms I’ve worked in, what’s the big deal with the warning sign on the door?”

Roger Kaiser shifted his weight suddenly to the other foot, surprised at the abruptness of that question. He was irritated that his new recruit had not responded in any way to the highly complimentary introduction that Roger had just given him about his aptitudes and patriotism. *He might at least,* Roger thought, *have thanked him for the compliments he had just gotten, or for the fact that he had just gotten a raise and a prestigious new job in national security.*

Because he was miffed, all Roger could think of was to reinforce his earlier introduction, so he answered, "Well, the law is the law, and we want everybody who works here to know up front that this is definitely deep security. We can't afford any leaks here of any sort. This is the type of work that you *can't* take home with you to your wife or girlfriend and discuss with them. And you've got to understand that from the get-go. As they used to say in World War II, 'Loose lips sink ships.' "

Karl was trying his best to follow this. But since he wasn't married yet at age thirty-one—he had never had time enough away from work to satisfy any one girl—he didn't have to worry about blabbing to someone at home. He lived alone in his apartment in Virginia. In addition, he wasn't ready to get married yet because he was still trying to pay back all of his college loans. And he wanted to put a little money in the bank before he got too serious with anyone.

As far as disclosing confidential information from work to his casual date, that just wasn't going to happen. He had always taken his responsibilities seriously. And he had always obeyed the law, both because it was his natural instinct, and also because he was practical. He never wanted to go to trial to defend himself against traffic or criminal charges. In fact, he actually had never received a single traffic ticket. That was mainly because he actually believed there was reason for all those traffic rules and laws. Thirty-five miles per hour meant there were pedestrians in the area that could get hurt, for instance. Those laws were there to keep him out of accidents, and to protect other people's lives. He had no problem with that.

So protecting government secrets was no problem for him either. But that left him a little puzzled. Why was his new boss lecturing him on what the agency already knew were strengths of his—his loyalty and honesty? Wasn't Roger Kaiser being a bit redundant?

So Karl just did the shuffle, saying, "Absolutely, we all know these are dangerous times and you just can't be too careful. We even have to be scrupulous about seemingly unimportant details when we are in high-security work."

That seemed to relieve Roger's nervousness a bit and he continued to go further into his set introduction. "Right on! I have to let all you new conscripts know where we stand, so we don't have any slip-ups. That's the reason for the warning on the sign. This is weighty and urgent stuff we're dealing with here."

Since Karl said nothing further, Roger then continued, "All I can do today is just show you the place. The actual work starts tomorrow at eight-thirty, right here in this room. Your job is called 'Security Tape Analyst,' and it's done right there at these computers. We have a computer set up for you right here, if you'd like to try it a bit."

As Karl sat down at the computer, his boss planted his hand on the back of Karl's chair and proceeded to turn on Karl's computer with his other hand. As he did so, an image started to appear on the monitor. Roger started to explain. "Most of the work here is done on computers, so you will be using yours on a daily basis. As usual, the power is provided by the CPUs over here. The work itself consists of your analysis of the 'simulation' which is now appearing on the screen. We will teach you, of course, how to do that analysis. It will provide you with an opportunity to utilize the reasoning and analytical skills for which you have been chosen. That is where you really get a chance to show your stuff!"

Then, apparently feeling that he had said enough for their first meeting, he decided to call it a day, with a jaunty, "Really not so tough now, is it? We'll get into it in more detail tomorrow."

II
A Choice Assignment at the Paper

A few hundred miles to the north, in New York City, John Bryce had been called into the office of the newspaper's editor-in-chief. John had just been told that the editor wanted to talk to him about a new assignment.

"John," the silver-haired editor stated abruptly, "we've got a tough assignment for you in Washington. Sit down and listen to what we've got in mind. Primarily, the situation down in D.C. has gotten very dicey. It looks as though the country may be headed for war, but the public still hasn't been informed. Since nobody has ever written any legal rules to be followed in carrying out a pre-emptive, unilateral military attack on a foreign, sovereign nation, a country about to conduct such an attack does not have to comply with any rules. At least, that is what we are afraid of. So we want to find out what is happening inside the beltway in Washington. We want to run a series of articles informing our readers of our concerns about the impending crisis.

"We need a reporter with top-notch skills in the international area, who can also go into the Washington, D.C. maze and come out with a story. Someone like a modern-day Daniel Schorr. We've decided to give you the assignment, unless you can give us a good reason why we shouldn't."

To John Bryce, this immediately sounded like the opportunity of a lifetime. Ever since getting out of journalism school he had thought about Professor Belcore's convictions—he could still remember the stentorian voice in which Belcore had addressed his class, "In this country, in this field, the opportunity is there every day. In this country, you can each decide whether to contribute to the betterment, or misery, of mankind. The decision will be up to each of you. You have to decide whether to be of assistance to your fellow Americans, or not to be. You will each make that decision by deciding where to work, what to write, and what not to write. You will be asked to aid both the cruel and expedient, and to assist the helpless and the weak. So be prepared."

As he quickly evaluated the situation and the opportunity that was apparently his for the asking, John thought it was all too simple. Of course there were risks. Perhaps they could "blackball" him, or try to, anyway. Or he could be investigated. They had tried to do that with Daniel Schorr, hadn't they? But they hadn't succeeded. And he knew he hadn't ever done anything criminally wrong, so they couldn't find anything even if they did investigate him, unless they invented it. So it was definitely thumbs up, oh yeah it was!

"Well, sir, it sounds like the assignment of a lifetime to me," he said. "Definitely count me in. When do I start?"

"Well, John, you're going to have to use all your experience, as well as any street smarts you've picked up, on this one," replied the editor. "We know you've only been in journalism for nine years, but we think you've got what it takes. We particularly like the firsthand experience you've had reporting on the wars in Somalia and Bosnia. You'll have to use all of your contacts, and every trick that you've ever learned to get that story out of Washington. We know this is not an easy assignment. In fact, it is a very difficult one. We want you to consult with all of our Washington crew, including the military beat—that would be Charlie Ball. And you're going to have to be in close contact with our in-house legal counsel, Dwight Percival, who is also in Washington. You're going to face some legal questions and issues that he can help you with.

"Bottom line, we want a series of three or four front-page articles in no less than three weeks, advising the public whether the Administration intends to go to war even if Congress and/or the U.N. turns down President Muller's request to make a 'regime change' in Razik. As for how you proceed, you'll have to discuss that with our Washington office. This will be your only assignment for the next three weeks, so you can set your own schedule.

"Good luck," he continued, "and deliver the copy to the Washington office in person. No faxes, no e-mail. We'd like to have you report back to the paper in two-and-a-half weeks, hopefully with some finished copy at that time."

John nodded in assent, said, "Okay, I've got it," stood up, and was out the door before the editor could offer him a "spot" of afternoon tea.

III
A Night Out

Karl Erskine skipped out of the Justice Buildings as quickly as possible; it was already past 5 P.M. and he had an early dinner date with Jill at 7:15 P.M. He strode across the street to the government parking lot and jumped into his old Pontiac Grand Prix, started the engine, and pulled out of the lot. As he left, he showed his pass to the security guard at the gate, then drove out onto Pennsylvania Avenue and headed west toward the Key Bridge and his apartment in Alexandria, Virginia.

After he arrived back at his apartment, it took him no more than twenty minutes to change into more casual attire, get back into his Pontiac again, and head north in Virginia to the Chain Bridge, which he crossed into the District of Columbia. Then he headed north into Maryland. Jill lived in Bethesda, Maryland, in a large brick apartment complex that was probably built shortly after World War II. For its time, it had all the modern conveniences, including a swimming pool, individual garages, adjoining verandas and yards, and recently remodeled kitchens and interiors. It was called Brunswick Arms and was just off of Wisconsin Avenue, just beyond Bradley Boulevard.

Jill was already at the door when he stepped out of his car. "Hi, Karl," she called from the door of her apartment, about thirty feet from where he was parked. She had a very wry smile encased in an otherwise slightly sad demeanor. A mid-level numbers analyst, she seemed pleased to see him. She came from a small town near Karl's own hometown of Richmond, Virginia. He had met her at a cocktail party in Georgetown about six months earlier, and he had been out with her perhaps three or four times, although he still did not feel that he knew her well.

As she got into his car he felt very pleased to have a chance to share her company on this warm summer evening in July, because she was friendly, quite sincere, and came from the same area as he. *The world is full of strangers,* he thought, *and it certainly seemed as if he had spent his entire day with some of them.* Plain and simple, it was good to finally be with someone that he could talk to in a meaningful way. Her occasional smile or low laugh, as they drove north out of Bethesda toward Rockville, Maryland, portended an enjoyable evening ahead.

He had decided to take her to a small, upscale restaurant in rural Maryland, about fifteen miles north of Rockville, and when he asked, she had concurred. The restaurant claimed, and also appeared to be, a holdover from the Revolutionary War period. It was an old stone tavern in the rolling farmland of northern Maryland, and was surrounded by large trees with branches drooping almost to the ground. At the entrance there was an engraved plaque containing the names of the famous generals and politicians who had dined there many years earlier, including General George Washington and Thomas Jefferson.

Jill and Karl were seated by the hostess in one of several small dining rooms. This particular room looked as if it used to be a living room from a still earlier log-dwelling house. Two walls of the dining room were lined with what appeared to be the original logs, which seemed to be held together by more recently added cement chinks. As a further testament to its authenticity, a narrow stone stairway led down from the room in which they were seated to a dark, sunken bar which, according to another plaque on the stairway, had been used as slave quarters up until the time of the Civil War. Jill seemed to wince slightly as she peered down into the darkened interior of the former slave hovel.

They shared a carafe of red Australian wine and both decided to order roast duckling, which turned out to be delicious. He told her that he had just received a promotion into national security work, and that a pay-raise went with it. Beyond that he told her nothing, except that the work was classified, top secret, and that as a result he could say no more about it. He did comment, though, that the new work looked interesting and challenging, and that it was important to the country.

She, on the other hand, told him that she had had terrible day. Her overbearing supervisor, a woman from accounting, had been on her back all day, complaining about everything. Jill related how the supervisor claimed to have a master's degree in personnel management, and therefore apparently felt that she had a right to tell everyone else how to do their job. Not surprisingly, her MO was to advise all her underlings that they were doing their work wrong. So she had told Jill that the formatting on her computer was completely outdated, and that she needed to install new software, which would probably take about three months to accomplish in-house.

Since Jill and Karl both had to get to work the following morning, they finished their light cup of decaf at about 9:30 P.M., and began to fold their napkins. Getting the message, the waitress soon delivered the bill, which Karl paid at the receptionist's desk on the way out. They got into his Pontiac and headed back toward Rockville and Bethesda.

Since it was almost dark, the traffic was relatively light, and they were able to make a rapid trip back to her apartment.

As he took her to the door, she thanked him for the evening. He responded that he had also had a very good time. Then he reached over, took her arm lightly, and gave her a light peck on the cheek. That seemed to stimulate a quick reaction from her. She suddenly stepped back, stiffened her back, raised her right arm halfway up to the sky, and then abruptly said "Heil" to him. Then she turned, stepped inside, briefly looked at him staring at her in disbelief, and shut the door in his face.

Astounded, he turned and walked slowly toward his car, trying to figure out what had just taken place. *Was she serious? How had he offended her? Was she some sort of kook? Was it a joke?*

But it was beyond him. He didn't understand. And he had to go. He just shook his head slowly as he got back into his Pontiac. She had seemed like such a nice, well-brought-up girl!

IV

A Promotion to the Pentagon

Newly promoted Lieutenant-Colonel Dan Dunphy presented his ID card to the female MP at the gatehouse of the Pentagon, and was waved on into the giant Pentagon building. Next he reported promptly to his new office in the War Plans Section. A West Point graduate, he had just gotten the best break of his fifteen-year career with the U.S. Army. He had been assigned to the prestigious War Plans Office and simultaneously promoted to the rank of lieutenant colonel.

His new assignment was to assist in the planning for a possible U.S. attack on the middle-eastern nation of Razik. When he had arrived at 7:55 A.M., the office was already packed with military personnel, primarily Army and Air Force. Adjacent to his desk was a large wall map of the Middle East, outlining the boundaries of Razik, Turkey, Iran, Syria, Saudi Arabia, Qatar, and Bahrain. It showed all the main highway routes, oil fields, airports and military installations of each nation, highlighted with appropriate military abbreviations and icons.

Dunphy's job was basically Army logistics—to assist planning the movements of troops, artillery, and materiel from bases in Kuwait, Poland, and Qatar into Razik in time to support fast-moving American and British tanks and armored personnel carriers moving into Razik. One unresolved contingency involved whether Israeli Army forces might attack on their own, or even join the U.S., so separate plans and calculations had to be made for that contingency as well. With the rank of lieutenant colonel, Dunphy served at the bottom of the hierarchy of high-ranking colonels and generals assigned to that unit.

V
Bryce Enters the Washington Maze

John Bryce wasted no time in getting the first flight out of JFK to National Airport in D.C., and immediately reported in to the newspaper's Washington office, where the *New York Times* military correspondent and in-house legal counsel were already waiting for him.

A conference had been pre-arranged for them by the Washington editor, and the conference room had been fully prepared. A jug of steaming hot coffee, sugar cubes and cream sat on a circular tray in the middle of a twelve-foot-long conference table. There was also a stack of legal-sized yellow pads and a 900-mgz portable phone that could be switched to speaker phone or conference calls if need be. The wooden conference table sat in a large, walnut-paneled conference room with a picture window that faced toward both the Reflecting Pool and Capitol Hill. It offered a panoramic view of the Lincoln Memorial on the west, along the full length of the Reflecting Pool to the glistening Congressional dome on the east. The interior wall of the conference room was also made of plate glass, and looked out onto a circular, spiral staircase which curled around in a side arc from the first floor of the building to the receptionist's desk on the second floor. Looking around, Bryce noticed that the second floor also housed the Washington office's morgue of old newspaper articles, and its own library.

Charles Ball, the paper's military correspondent, and Dwight Percival, the in-house legal counsel, were already sipping their cups of coffee and talking back and forth when John Bryce entered the room. "Hello, John," piped Charlie Ball, "you've got yourself a real hot potato on this one. Hope you don't get burned."

Charlie had been a real "find" for the *Times*. A former military officer, he had joined the army as a ROTC officer out of Ohio State and had been assigned to the U.S. Army Press Corps, and had spent twenty years reporting news for the *Stars and Stripes* before becoming its editor. After retiring as a full colonel, he had been hired by the *Times*. He was a highly experienced reporter, who also had extensive knowledge of the military, and he had now been a premiere reporter for the *Times* for three years.

"John, we've been mapping out where you've got to go on this one," continued Charlie. "However you slice it, you're going to have to get inside the Pentagon to see what our military Goliath there is up to. But you're going to have to be very careful. Daniel Ellsberg learned that back in the seventies. We'd rather get this information cleanly, if it can be done, but the boss says we're going to back you all the way on this. It is very important to the people of this country, and to this newspaper, to get this information about U.S. intentions with respect to Razik out to the public. So if you get into trouble on this, the paper will make its full resources available to you. If we have another *Times v. United States* to get this story out, so be it. Dwight will give you a survey of the applicable legal traps, so you can keep your eye out for them. After you talk to someone in the Pentagon, we also want you to get in touch with a contact that we have on the House Intelligence Committee.

"John, we don't want you to get sandbagged on this," Dwight then cautioned, "so you're going to have to watch out for a number of provisions of the National Security Act, Foreign Intelligence Surveillance Act, and the U.S. Patriot Act, as well as the general criminal provisions, unfortunately, of the U.S. Code. And, generally, it would also be helpful to know a little historical background, which you could obtain by reading a biography on Daniel Schorr and Daniel Ellsberg, the famous duo from the 1970s. In fact, I recommend that you review Schorr's own autobiography, *Staying Tuned* for a laundry list of all the possible legal problems that you might run into while working on this assignment. I also recommend that you read about Ellsberg's accomplishments in K.W. Salter's *The Pentagon Papers Trial* at the nearest library. Or, if you don't want to leave a paper trail at the local public library—remember the FBI can now come into any public library and get a list of the books you've taken out—the paper's own library here in this building has most of these books right here on the second floor.

"And if your memory of the 1970s is still not too sharp, you might also try checking on all our news stories on the subject of Watergate. We also have copies of all our own news stories at the paper's morgue on this floor. We're going to give you four days just to catch up on that material.

"But remember, mum's the word on your activities down here in this snakepit. You don't have the same mores here that you do in New York City. There are no 'old school' customs here to protect you. As you should know, anything goes in this town, and anybody you talk to in the government could be looking to set you up for a perjury lesson before a congressional committee, or for a grand jury appearance in the *Pentagon Papers II* case, so stay alert at all times.

"But, by the same token, don't forget that the First Amendment proved to be strong enough to protect both the

Pentagon Papers and Dan Ellsberg in the end in the 1970s. The 'prior restraint' injunction against publishing those Viet Nam-era military secrets was reversed, and thrown out, by the U.S. Supreme Court in 1971. And the government also ended up dropping the criminal charges against Dan Ellsberg. We project the same result now with the current Supreme Court if the issue should ever go that far at this time. Even though Congress has the right to pass stringent laws with respect to protecting national security secrets, the federal courts can still review such laws on appeal and throw out any criminal convictions based on violating these laws, if it decides that your work and writing are protected under the First Amendment.

"The Constitution never envisioned the United States as an ironclad ship of state that would use its heavy armor to plow through an unsuspecting and defenseless public. Remember the *Monitor* and *Merrimac* during the Civil War. They were both ironclad ships that were supposed to ram and sink other ships. One sailed for the Union, and the other for the Confederacy. But it didn't work out to either side's advantage in the war. Since both sides had these new weapons, they offset each other, and really had no effect on the ultimate outcome of the war.

"And the Supreme Court has already written the textbook on the subject of freedom of the press, as it applies to your freedom to obtain and publish classified documents that the public has a legitimate interest in reading, during the *Pentagon Papers* case, as I mentioned, *New York Times v. U.S.* in the 1970s. I expect no less of a victory for the First Amendment now from an equally distinguished Supreme Court, if the issue were to come up again.

"An imperious ship of state," he continued, "will always be torpedoed by the High Court if they get a chance, because the Supreme Court has the most to lose from an etatist administration trying to throw its weight around in Washington." Apparently now satisfied with his closing, the in-house counsel leaned back slightly in his chair, and appeared to rest his case.

VI
Through the Looking Glass

Anxious to find out more about his new assignment, Karl Erskine appeared early at his office the next day, and went directly to the National Security cubbyhole. A group of four other employees, all apparently newly assigned to their high security positions, also sat down at their assigned computers, while a senior employee readied his notes at a temporary podium at the front of the room.

A burly senior employee of about forty, who appeared to be about five-feet-eight-inches tall, introduced himself as Sam Silovich, and began to speak in a low voice, gesturing with both hands and head periodically in an emphatic manner. As he talked, his beady eyes moved from one new person to the next, as if to gauge their response to his words. "Hello, folks," he ventured. "Congratulations on being selected for this new, top-secret assignment. The competition for these assignments has been very intense, so you have a right to be proud as being selected. Many applicants did not make it. Unfortunately, you will have to be satisfied with the esteem and recognition that you will receive from your fellow workers here, because you cannot—repeat, *cannot*—inform anyone else of your selection, any more than you can tell them about anything else that you do or learn from this assignment.

"To start, I would like you to turn on the CPUs and the

monitors in front of you. Then go to the logo for GovSec, and then observe the simulation which will appear on the monitor. You will note that there are various activities going on there—things taking place on the screen—live action, so to speak, with people moving around and talking. After looking at those activities for a couple of minutes, please describe in conclusory form on the yellow pads placed in front of you what you are seeing. If you can't figure out what you are seeing, then draw your conclusions negatively, thus describing what you are not viewing. Please begin now. Thank you."

Karl Erskine switched on the CPU unit on the floor next to him, and then flicked on the monitor. Then he located the special Gov.Sec. logo as it formed on the screen. Next he moved the cursor to the that logo and pressed twice. Soon a rather ordinary-looking scene appeared on the screen. A picture of a room, which looked like somebody's living room, with a man sitting on a couch and a woman leaning back in a reclining chair of some sort. Although the man appeared to be talking to the woman, there was no audible sound. Their body language and movements were visible, but there were no voices to be heard. It was almost like an old silent movie, but without any subtitles. After studying the scene for a moment, Karl started to write down his observations in longhand.

"It appears that we are watching an ordinary couple sitting and talking in their living room. Since I can't tell much more without hearing the sound of their voices, I can only say that this is not some kind of TV drama because there are no advertisements. Also, it is not a sitcom because the people seem to be dead serious and nobody laughs. And it does not appear to be a quiz show because the stage-setting is wrong, and it does not appear that anyone is asking or answering questions. It could be a surveillance film, perhaps like the ones shown on *60 Minutes* or *Candid Camera.* It is really sort of like a silent film without subtitles. That is about all I can figure out at this point."

As Sam Silovich collected the papers from the new recruits, he stressed that the basic nature of this work required the analysts to learn to use their own minds, and to think on the job. "We want our people to learn to draw deductions as they work, and to read between the lines. The way you think is important to us. Your attitudes are also important, so we get you into this material slowly. That way we can develop good lines of communication between us from the get go."

That completed, he then launched into a new tack with what appeared to be a prepared speech or dissertation: "It is very important for you to understand thoroughly," he reiterated, "the classified nature of this work and technology. The job function itself, as well as the functions performed here, are both classified. This is a so-called 'black area' of government. As far as the government is concerned, your job here actually does not exist, nor does the technology that sits in front of you. If the government is ever asked, it would deny that this technology, or that your jobs even exist, because both are classified and thus obviously secret." As if intrigued by this legal fiction, he then continued with a slight smile, "As you know, if someone were to disclose the existence of this work, then it would no longer be secret, would it? So we can't let that happen, can we?" he added, purposefully.

"By the same token," he continued, "if one of you were to ask for more information about this job than we provide you with, once again we could not answer your questions because the information that you were asking about would undoubtedly be classified. Obviously, in that situation you are not entitled to any more information than we give you. So please, let's not ask any unnecessary questions. We will definitely give you all the information that you need in order to do your jobs properly," he concluded.

"Basically, we are involved in collecting information that will be used for national security purposes by other branches of government. However, as I have said, the method or means by which you do your job is definitely classified and cannot be disclosed by you to anyone. That is why we have placed the warning signs on the door going into this room. The penalties for disclosing such information to the outside are also set forth on the warning sign just inside the door. Those penalties, as I am sure you have already noticed, are very severe. Needless to say, we have had no one break these secrecy rules." Then, launching into his subject matter with new enthusiasm, he added, "You should definitely understand, though, that we are decidedly not doing anything illegal here. Nor are we hiding anything illegal from the public. Our procedures are all conducted pursuant to laws that have already been passed by Congress. In fact, the underpinning to this work—FISA, or the Foreign Intelligence Surveillance Act—was passed by Congress way back in 1978, and signed into law by none other than President Jimmy Carter. That statute creates and legalizes the veil of secrecy that we work behind here in this room.

"In a sense, you might say that what you see here is all a trade secret owned by the government itself. In fact, you will receive a lecture later, from an attorney from this office that will provide you with a more detailed description of the legal underpinnings of our secret work here."

Thusly, Sam Silovich applied an atomization theory to the work he had been explaining to his new recruits. *That theory,* he thought smugly to himself, *further served to pro-*

tect the noble governmental purpose of fighting terrorism. By dividing up national security work into assembly line-like components, and then creating a wall around each component person in the chain of production, and prohibiting each person collecting information for the government from asking about how the information was later used, or about the process as a whole, it was impossible for any one employee to understand what was going on. After all, there was no terrorist like a dead terrorist. Sometimes he even wondered if some of his most critical superiors in government—higher up the chain and closer to the president—were not also terrorist sympathizers. Perhaps they too would get their just desserts some day!

Since nobody in the room with him knew how the information was collected in the first place, or how it was used later, they were all kept in the dark about the government's covert operations in this country.

His mission for the day apparently completed, he then decided to dispatch his recruits for the day, "That's about it for today. You can now return to your old jobs for the remainder of the day and finish up there on any work that you still have left. But I want you to think about our new work and what I've told you here today. As you can probably see now, classified work may be quite different from your old work. The procedures and atmosphere may also be quite a bit different. And if you don't feel comfortable in this new environment, or if this new work goes against the grain with you in some way, we'd really like to know about it now! So please, feel free to give me or Roger Kaiser a ring, or stop in and see us, and tell us if that is the case. At this point, we could probably get you returned to your old job without any damage to your standing there.

"But please understand, this is the last time that you can opt out of this new assignment. From now on, you'll just have to grin and bear it, and serve out your assigned tour of duty here. We can't waste further time and money on your training here, and then have you transferred back to your old jobs later.

"So," he concluded, "any questions? If not, see you here tomorrow morning, same time, same station."

As he left the room, Karl Erskine was puzzled and somewhat troubled about the exact nature of the national security work that he was going to be doing in this new office. But, as an experienced member of the bureaucracy, he was careful not to leave any telltale signs on his face or in his comments to his cohorts as he left the room.

VII
Bryce Approaches the Pentagon

John Bryce had been around the newspaper business for quite a while. He knew how to follow-up on leads and track down a story. He had done that in looking for grave sites in Bosnia and Kosovo. Ordinarily he could track down information in any environment. He had started out as a foreign correspondent with the *Times* right out of journalism school at Columbia. He only had three weeks of orientation with the *Times* before getting his first assignment to go to Somalia as a foreign correspondent. His job there was to cover the aftermath of the American attack on Somalia in 1993. That had been a tough assignment. He, and the other member of the press corps who had been admitted into the country by the Somalis, had felt vulnerable and threatened the whole time they were there. It had seemed that they were only allowed into the country in the first place so that the American press would get enough coverage of the shocking defeat of the American force after it attacked Somalia, and sufficiently graphic pictures of the captured G.I.s who were dragged through the streets in various stages of undress by the Somali warlords. After that, he had gotten assignments in London, Dublin, and Moscow, and had even covered the Civil War in Bosnia and Kosovo. But this latest assignment in Washington, which was almost certainly the most significant of his career, was also turning out to be the most difficult. After one week in Washington, D.C., he had not developed a single lead. Following instructions form the Washington office of the *Times,* he had lunched with various important people at the Washington Hilton, the cafeteria of the Museum of Modern Art, the Marriott Inn in Arlington, and even at the Congressional dining room. He had met with various employees on Capitol Hill, "think tank" experts in Washington on the Middle East, well-connected lawyers in private practice in D.C., and had even met with several astute reporters from other newspapers, but nobody had any answers. They were not sure what President Muller planned to do.

They did not know what the Administration would do if the United Nations Security Council refused to authorize an attack on Razik. Nor what the U.S. Congress would do if the war resolution pending before the Security Council was vetoed by another permanent member of the council, which was a good possibility. What would we do if the U.N. opted instead for more inspections, in order to determine if Razik had stored large quantities of weapons of mass destruction, as alleged by President Muller? Would the U.S. attack anyway, even without U.N. approval? Was the mass deployment of American troops to the Persian Gulf intended as a threat to persuade Razik to permit renewed U.N. inspections or, on the contrary, did it mean that the U.S. had already made up its mind and intended to go to war even if the U.N. refused to approve their planned attack? John could find no answers to these questions.

One week after receiving his original marching order in the Washington Office of the *Times,* he was forced to call in and advise Charlie Ball that he had run into a stone wall and could find no credible evidence upon which to base a story. The military correspondent was not caught off guard, though, and did not seem terribly surprised. He had an immediate suggestion for Bryce. "Hopefully," he suggested, "I've got a way out of this maze for you. There's a military guy from Desert Storm who has just been promoted to a slot at the Pentagon in War Plans, and he has got to know if an immediate attack is planned for Razik. If the president has already decided to attack, the Army has got to know about it so they can draw up their plans to move troops and material in time. His name is Lieutenant-Colonel Dan Dunphy. Let me give him a ring and see if I can get an appointment for you to see him."

Bryce liked the idea and immediately accepted the offer. So Ball left the room in order to use his private telephone. He returned in about ten minutes with a reply. "Dunphy says okay, but you'll have to meet him on the way home, not at the Pentagon. Since he walks home through the Arlington Cemetery, he could meet you at the entrance of the cemetery on the side of the Pentagon, and then walk with you to his house in Arlington on the other side. It takes him about twenty minutes in all. He says he is willing to try to help out but it depends on what you are looking for in the way of information. No promises, you know."

"Terrific, that's fine with me," Bryce retorted quickly. "Maybe we have finally gotten a break. Ask him of we can do it tomorrow, and, if so, at what time?"

Charlie Ball went back to the phone and quickly returned with a time of 5:30 P.M. for the next afternoon.

The next day, Bryce arrived early at the side entrance to the Arlington Cemetery, which was about a mile from the gigantic structure of the five-sided Pentagon which he could see in the distance. As he arrived he could see an Army officer coming down the sidewalk from the direction of the Pentagon, and he guessed it was probably Lieutenant-Colonel Dunphy, because he seemed to be looking directly ahead in Bryce's direction with a quizzical look on his face.

As it turned out, the clean-cut-looking Army officer coming toward him from the Pentagon was, in fact, Dan Dunphy. Bryce guessed him to be about forty years old. Dan shook Bryce's hand vigorously as he introduced himself, and pointed toward the path across the cemetery to his house. "You really could say," he joked as they started across the cemetery to his house, "that I know where all the bodies are buried around here. That doesn't mean I can tell you about it, but I'll see what I can do."

As Bryce struggled to keep up with the quick stride of the Army officer, he got right to the point, "Well, I'm really not looking for any dirt on the Pentagon. All I'm trying to find out for the *Times* is the direction of the Administration's military policy in the Middle East. Specifically, if the U.N. refuses to approve any military action against Razik, will the U.S. accept the Security Council's position, or will we attack Razik preemptively on our own?"

As he caught the question, Captain Dunphy seemed to break stride for a moment, and then abruptly put his hand up and pushed back his military beret, and started to scratch his forehead. "Well, isn't that a jim-dandy of a question? Isn't that kind of a tough way for me to end a long day, trying to answer a question like that?" he snapped.

After thinking for a moment as he continued to walk briskly, he started to talk slowly, "I guess I'll have to answer that with a little story. You see, there once was a young cadet from Pine Bluff, Idaho who received the honor of a congressional appointment to West Point. While there, he worked his butt off for four years in hopes of graduating. He hoped to follow the Long Gray Line of cadets who gone before him, go out into a very tough world, and make a contribution and do a little good for his country. His goal was to follow the West Point motto of 'Duty, Honor, Country.' Eventually, he did graduate and later served in Desert

Storm. Still later, he was assigned to the Pentagon. And that's me.

"But, unfortunately, what you are asking me to do doesn't fit in with 'Honor.' I realize what you are requesting may be very honorable and useful for a journalist, but the information is still classified. And I am duty-bound to tell you that I can't reveal that information to you. Now, if you asked me to tell you about the soldier's life during Desert Storm, I could do that. But I can't give you the answer to the question that you asked me, even if I did know it."

"Well," persisted Bryce, "could you give me any explanation for the re-activation of the National Guard and Reserve units?"

"I can only say," responded Dunphy quickly, "that those units have been called up based on the orders of the Secretary of Defense, based on the perception of the intelligence community that we have a serious situation in the Middle East to deal with." Dunphy spoke with a slight cautionary tone in his voice, as he seemingly reverted to his serious, official demeanor.

Seemingly undaunted, John Bryce gave his mission one more try, "Would you be willing to comment on the troop build-up in Kuwait and Qatar?"

Finally closing the door for good, Lieutenant Colonel Dunphy then retorted, "No, I don't think that would be a very smart thing for a junior officer in the Pentagon to do. Sorry pal, but that's all I can do for you on this one."

"Yeah, perhaps some other time." Bryce nodded dolefully. "Well, it's been a pleasure meeting you anyway. Best of luck," Bryce concluded as he turned back and headed toward his parked car. *Another blind alley,* he mused, and his battery was beginning to wear down as well. *Maybe I should be devoting more time to getting in shape, rather than working on this Rubik's Cube of an assignment. I just don't seem to be getting anywhere. I simply can't get any hard facts on which to base a story.*

As he pondered his next step, he noticed that he was being watched by a middle-aged man hunched down behind the wheel in a car parked about fifty yards beyond his own on Cemetery Road. He appeared to be following Bryce's progress out of the cemetery and out onto the sidewalk with a fixed gaze. But every time Bryce made a point of looking directly at him, he would turn his head and look in a different direction. Just as Bryce reached his car, the middle-aged man in the car pulled out of his parking place and onto the street, giving Bryce one last darting gaze as he drove by him.

Interesting, thought Bryce. *Had he attracted the attention of some spook by meeting with a military officer in that manner? If so, whose spook was he? Was he foreign or domestic, and if the latter, FBI, CIA, NSA, Army or Navy Intelligence, or what?* Well, he had been warned before he took this assignment. Anyway, in three more days he was finally going to get a chance to return to Scarsdale and see his wife again, so he would be able to get some relief from this weird atmosphere.

But then, as Bryce himself got into his car and pulled out into the curving, tree-lined roadway only a mile or so from the Pentagon, a fast-moving, small, gray car came toward him from the opposite direction. When it was about seventy-five yards away, Bryce noticed that the driver suddenly seemed to lean forward and to his right inside the car. As he did so, his oncoming car suddenly swerved to the left directly toward Bryce's car. But at the last minute it suddenly swerved back and away from Bryce's car, and buzzed by him. *Very peculiar,* Bryce thought. *No traffic conditions to cause that behavior. Too many loony birds on the highway, I guess.*

VIII
Using "Radar" at the Office

The following morning as Karl Erskine turned the corner of the hallway on the fifth floor of the Justice Building and headed toward the Audio-Visual Room of the Foreign Counter-Intelligence Office, he had finally resolved any doubts that he had about his new assignment. He was going forward. His curiosity had, perhaps, always been his greatest enemy, he thought, and it was not helping him any here. He definitely wanted to get to the bottom of this mystery, and find out what this new job was about. Why were they keeping it so mysterious, and why were the penalties so great for disclosing anything about it?

In addition, the higher grade rating on his new job, and the higher salary that went with it, were also important to him. The extra $150 he would receive each week would allow him to pay off his college debt in another ten months, so he would be financially a free man again, after fourteen years of indebtedness.

As Karl entered the room and took his seat behind his computer monitor, the swarthy supervisor from the day before, Sam Silovich, was once again swinging into a talk. "Well, I'm glad to see all of you new recruits are back again! Today you will have a rare treat—an opportunity to see, and be in on, a new governmental technology at work. This is the cutting edge of applied science—new computer and telecommunications technologies being merged to create a new tool for the government to use.

"Today you, in a sense, fall into one of those rare groups of people who have the privilege of seeing the future. Just as members of the court of Ferdinand and Isabella saw the opportunity to prove that the world was not flat by launching Columbus on his trip to America, you will have the opportunity to work on a revolutionary new process. As you use this process, you will see how it separates you from the rest of our countrymen, because you will see how outdated their thinking has become. Just as Columbus's sponsors perceived that the thinking of their countrymen was backward and obsolete you will see the new forces shaping our democracy.

"Please turn on your computer and hit the Gov.Sec. icon."

As Karl Erskine turned on the Internet service provided and logged on to Gov.Sec., he watched as another picture appeared, similar to the one he had seen on his first day of orientation. This time the man on the screen appeared to be sitting at a metal kitchen table, where he was eating some kind of food together with a somewhat plump-looking woman, perhaps his wife or girlfriend. Due to the modern and plush furniture and decor, and the yuppie-like appearance of the couple, he judged them to be middle-class Americans. But this time there was a big difference in the tape. There were now voices, and he could hear the guy talking with the woman.

The couple seemed to be alternately talking with each other, and then looking in the direction of the camera that was apparently taping them. Karl could also hear a voice which sounded like a man giving the morning news in New York City. He was describing a parade on Fifth Avenue and some crowds that had been demonstrating and acting up at Times Square.

When the couple talked they seemed to be upset about something. The man was saying that he had to go back to Washington for one more week. Things were not going as he had hoped. But the paper was giving him one more week to come up with a story with something definite with respect to Razik.

At that point in Karl's work, the instructor, Sam Silovich, interrupted his recruits with some further instructions. "All right, now that you've seen it, please turn your monitor off for a moment. I need to give you further instructions.

"Okay now, this is your first exposure to a full tape with both sound and video. This is a real case, where we're operating with a court order. This is also your point of no return. Consider yourself officially 'in,' as we say, from this point forward. We cannot transfer you back to your old job from this point on. We have too much invested in your training to do that. Your instructions are as follows," he continued. "Take down all the information on your yellow pads, as requested on the instruction sheet that I am now passing out. The purpose of taking down the specified information is to create an outline or summary of the information contained on the tape you are reviewing, so that the next person working on that tape has an index of the contents of the tape, and can locate any specific information quickly without reviewing the whole tape. Or, if necessary, he or she will know where to go to get a copy of the original taped version.

"As you listen to the tape that you are analyzing and observe the gestures of the various 'subjects' being taped, please note the following information that you observe or hear: Any political statements made by the subject, quote as accurately as possible exactly what is said by the 'subject' and on what political topic. Also, please put down any references to any political affiliations that are revealed in the conversations. Note the names of any other persons mentioned in any political discussion, and the location of any future political discussions that are to be held in the future. Please remember that under Patriot Act Section 214 the department can go after targets based in part on statements of opinion that would otherwise be protected under the First Amendment to the Constitution. In addition, the attorney-general's guidelines permit us to attend meetings which are solely political in nature even though there is no suspicion of terrorism or any other violation of the law involved. Of course, should you hear anything on the tapes about any planned terrorist attack or activities, or any planned used of force to achieve political objectives, also make a note of that.

"Secondly, please note all matters related to any planned travel, particularly to any foreign country, or any socially oriented travel, such as traveling out to eat somewhere. If the subject plans any trip out of the country, or in the country, please note the date, time, and place of departure and planned itinerary, if it is discussed on the tapes.

"And if the 'subjects' are planning to meet with any other person on the trip, please note all possible information about such person or persons as well, including their addresses, place of employment, etc. As for socially oriented travel, please note the time, place, date, and of course, the name of the restaurant. This will enable us to conduct appropriate surveillance in person, if necessary, with appropriate recording devices.

"Thirdly, as to health matters, please note the nature of any physical ailment, and the name and address of the treating physician, since we now have the right to demand copies of all medical records from the doctor under Section 215 of the Patriot Act. Also note the name of the medical insurance carrier and address of same. Note the time and place of any medical appointments if you hear them mentioned on the tapes. Note in particular any form of psychiatric or psychological treatments being received by the subjects or any hospitalizations for same. Furthermore, please feel free to detail any form of expression or behavior of the subject which, in your opinion, evidences any existing psychological condition. For instance, if the subject shows any form of sexual exhibitionism, such as a woman who wears revealing or skimpy clothing around the house, please note the same.

"As to the subject's deportment, please note any known sexual habits, leanings, or proclivities, either as seen on the tapes or referred to in conversation, and the names of any known sexual partners, particularly if outside any marital relationship.

"As to any financial matters, kindly note the names of any bank or stock brokerage firm used by the subject, or any planned transfer of any assets, particularly if the transfer is to go out of the country. Also note any references by the subject to any plans to sell any stock, particularly if the stock is to be sold in any company headed by any person who is known to communicate regularly with the subject. Also note any references to debt, credit card debt, or outstanding mortgages, as well as any forthcoming balances due on such debts. Note the names of any creditors.

"If the subject exhibits any form of personality trait, such as boastfulness, prevarication, or a markedly aggressive personality, please feel free to use your skills and training in that area to categorize such traits.

"To complete the subject's social profile, as you listen to the tapes, please note the names of all organizations or churches to which he or she belongs, and the times, locations and tenor of such meetings of such organizations, if known. Remember we are now permitted to send agents to church and religious meetings under the current guidelines of the attorney-general.

"And, of course, please note any references on the tapes to any violations of the law, such as any traffic tickets received by the subject, or any planned future violations of the law, particularly relating to any known or possible future violations of the internal revenue code.

"And that is basically it for the day," Silovich finally concluded, noting that his recruits were beginning to droop in their chairs a bit, and some were staring into space.

Somewhat startled at the abrupt ending of the labyrinthine list of information that they were supposed to write down, Karl Erskine got up slowly, stretched, and turned to leave the room. As he did so, he almost ran into Roger Kaiser, who had, unbeknownst to him, been sitting several seats behind him. Simultaneously, Roger patted Karl on the arm and said, "Hey, why don't we grab some lunch in about an hour?"

"Sounds good to me," Karl replied, "I do need something to break out of the mood," he continued. "It has been pretty confining here, hasn't it?"

Roger nodded and said, "We'll talk about that later," and then turned in the other direction and started to walk over to his own office.

An hour later, Karl and Roger walked across the street to one of the best little restaurants in Washington, one which was frequented by people from all the government agencies in the neighborhood, "Hogan's Salad Bar." After waiting at the door for about two minutes to be seated, they were led to a booth with high wooden backs over on the far side of the room. As they slid into their bench seats they noted the usual crowd of men and women in the restaurant with their gray, black and brown business suits and dresses, all seemingly deeply engrossed in fast-paced discussions with each other.

Both Roger and Karl made the decision to order a glass of California wine, hoping to ease the pressures of the day. The waitress then chirped that the special for the day was broiled haddock with Mussolini sauce. But they both elected to try the salad bar instead.

After settling back into their seats with full plates, Roger purposefully and quickly took the conversational lead. He asked Karl what he thought about his new assignment. Karl paused before responding, "Well, I'm not exactly sure where it's going, but I'd have to say it is not exactly what I'd been expecting."

Apparently not surprised, Roger countered quickly, "That's the way it is supposed to be. You are not supposed to anticipate what this job is going to be all about. It involves working with new governmental technology which is still unknown to the general public. In fact, the technology didn't even exist ten years ago. It is a melding of recent developments in television, radio-wave, and computer technologies and represents an effort by the government to catch up with recent strides in the electronics industry."

After pausing to gauge the mood and reaction of his recruit, he went on, "Karl, since I know you have a good theoretical mind, I think it might be helpful for me to give you the big picture here, before you jump to any hasty conclusions here about Sam Silovich's remarks earlier this morning. Do you remember the determinists philosophers from the 1960s? They argued that people could all be controlled by their environments, and that it was unrealistic to believe that people in the modern era were in any sense masters of their own fate. In reality, their entire lives were, or could be, controlled by others, and events that were beyond their control. Determinists basically contended that if one were to know everything about an individual, one could then predict and control the actions of that person. Thus, if the government had the ability to learn or find out everything about a person, then the government could even project the future actions of that individual, and perhaps even nip future troublemakers, like Thomas Paine, in the bud, or preemptively.

"In the 60s and 70s some scholars even contemplated that people's entire lives might be controlled by high-powered drugs and toxins. But," he continued, "even though these utopian notions were noxious, these philosophers were not too far off the mark in recognizing that some sort of control was, in fact, necessary in this country. And, technologically, it soon became apparent that a better way to control the fringe was soon available—control by the use of information alone. Information about each person, if sufficiently complete, was actually a means of control over those same persons.

"Certain people in this country, the determinists apparently felt, could not be allowed to pursue their own selfish aims, particularly when their objectives were totally inconsistent with those already in control of society. Thus, the need to control and regulate the excesses of individuals in our society would, of necessity, yield a new crop of investigative tools—in particular, secret methods of extrapolating information from the minds of the masses of Americans, and from individuals that they opposed. The extrapolated knowledge could then be put to use for the benefit of America as a whole. Yes, the government should, the people of this persuasion felt, soon be able to meld the knowledge of the people into the great common purpose, if you will—the very same purpose that they themselves espoused. Ultimate control was now possible."

Erskine, dumbfounded by his boss's sudden apostolic reverie, wondered to himself whether it had been brought on by the now-empty glass of wine. But he was not naive, and thus did not display a trace of surprise. He merely noted perfunctorily, "Well, I'm not up to date on philosophical matters but I've certainly seen a lot of people in this country do a lot of foolish things in recent years. And, obviously, the government can't be expected to stand pat in its ways and then be circumvented by human ingenuity and new technological development. In a rapidly changing environment, we obviously have to stay up to date, too."

But even as he was saying this, he thought to himself—*Is this real? Could this really be happening? Are there people in this world who actually think like this? Could his new boss be one of them?* Frankly, he wished he could forget the day—and in fact the whole new job—from Silovich's speech in the morning to Roger Kaiser's apparent view of the macrocosm. Was his boss actually trying to suggest that the government could—and should—get information out of people's heads without them knowing about it? If so, how was the government actually doing that?

The answer was not long in arriving. Perhaps surveillance tapes, which were probably what they had been watching under Silovich's tutelage during the morning, were part of that answer. Of course, nobody told him that those video tapes they had been watching were actually surveillance tapes, but what else could they be? But if they were, he still could not figure out how they could get into people's home to film those tapes without the owners and residents even knowing it. But since he knew he was not supposed to ask any questions, he had to accept the fact that he wasn't going to get any answers while talking further with Roger.

"Yes," nodded Roger, breaking Karl out of his own reverie, "we do have to keep up with the times and that is what your new job is about. I'm glad you understand."

But then, noting that he had apparently lost the attention of his younger cohort once again, Roger Kaiser wondered whether his new recruit might doubt the efficacy of his remarks. This, in turn, caused Roger to lose his own train of thought. As a result, he added pointedly, "Well, if this all seems like just theory to you, you should also understand that we don't just rely on our knowledge of these people for our 'muscle.' We turn our information over to the enforcement agencies, you know, and they get the results. And if they can't find anything, which is often the case, then we pass our information off to the state and local authorities for them to use as they see fit. Last, but not least, if something hasn't already happened, we then leave things to another law—the Law of Nature—Survival of the Fittest. And for that situation, we also have the 'spy in the sky,' but that doesn't relate to your work so I can't tell you about that."

Caught up in his own adrenalin, Roger then sputtered, "Believe me, it really works. You're just damn lucky to be on this end of the stick. I hope you appreciate it!" Then he suddenly stopped to study Karl and became worried about the inconclusive expression on Karl's face. Then Roger Kaiser finally decided that he had said too much. So he picked up the check, stood up abruptly, and headed quickly toward the cash register. Karl Erskine dutifully followed, not knowing if he was about to suffer from acute dyspepsia or merely dropsy of the spirit.

* * *

A full week had passed. The build-up of American troops in Qatar continued. War games were underway in the desert. The U.S. Congress had passed resolutions authorizing a military intervention in Razik to prevent a further build-up of weapons of mass destruction there. But the U.N. Security Council had refused to authorize a strike against Razik, largely because some nations questioned whether there still were any weapons of mass destruction in that country. So the intentions of the U.S. administration were still not evident. And President Muller definitely was not telegraphing his moves. So Bryce still sought doggedly to ascertain whether the U.S. actually intended to go to war.

* * *

IX
Caught in the Net on Capitol Hill

After his return to Washington on the following Monday, Bryce doggedly pursued his quest for other possible sources of information about the Administration's intentions in Razik.

His next step in that pursuit was Capitol Hill. Some of the staff people at the paper had some connections with the House Intelligence Committee. The newspaper's staffers were on a lunch-and-poker basis with Jake Reinwater, a legal assistant for the intelligence committee. A Republican, Reinwater had also acted in the past as a useful go-between for the committee and the paper. When the Intelligence Committee needed to get newspaper coverage, he could usually deliver space for an article in the *Washington Times*. In return, when the paper needed background information for an editorial on some trouble spot in the world or a fast-forward on the nature of some upcoming world event, Jake could usually accommodate them with the needed information. So John Bryce's phone call to Reinwater did not come as any great surprise to Jake, and he quickly agreed to have lunch with Bryce at the congressional cafeteria the next day.

As Bryce approached the office of the senior congressman from Wyoming in the Congressional Office Building the following morning, he could see that a fortyish-looking man in a gray suit and tie was already leaning against the wall next to the congressman's doorway, apparently reading the morning's newspaper. Since his short, clipped hair and six foot height met the description given to Bryce at the paper, he walked right up to him, offered his right hand and introduced himself as the *Times* reporter that had spoken with Reinwater earlier. The two of them then immediately made tracks to the elevator and then took the underground train ride to the congressional cafeteria. Along the way, after beginning with some brief chatter about the onset of the rainy season in the District of Columbia, John apprised Reinwater of the problem that brought him to Capitol Hill.

As Bryce talked about his paper's concern about a possible preemptive attack on Razik, he could see that Reinwater, who nodded often but said little, was both analyzing him, and also analyzing the request for information that Bryce was presenting to him.

Can I do anything, Reinwater wondered to himself, *to help Bryce? Do I actually have any of the information that Bryce apparently wants? Should I help him? Is the information classified? Would Congressman Dunder give me the okay to release any information to this particular reporter? If so, would it still be an illegal leak, for which I might be the ultimate fall guy?* This was definitely a tough one. *What do I really know about the intentions of the president myself?* This required some thought. Why, this guy wasn't even a regular player on the Washington scene.

In fact, why should I further this guy's career? What could he do in return? What would the New York City office of the Times *do for me, or for the intelligence committee?* Bryce had said nothing about that; not even any innuendo. *Just talking those infernal principles again. Not even any chance to win any bets later at the poker table with this guy.*

He wouldn't even be in Washington. Moreover, Bryce doesn't appear to be like a poker player. More like a crammer who always talked to the professors after class, and then later didn't have time for a beer after work. Yeah, this is a guy who is really after a Pulitzer Prize anyway, and *doesn't know how things really work nowadays! Probably even a dumb guy as far as National Security is concerned! Well, I don't have time to bring him up to date.*

After he bade Bryce farewell as they left the congressional dining room, he had another thought. One of the reasons he hadn't disclosed anything to Bryce—about the intentions of the Administration to go to war or not—was because he really didn't have any hard information himself on that subject. As far as he knew, the Intelligence Committee itself was having trouble getting any information from the White House on that subject. It seemed like the White House did not take kindly to inquiries from Capitol Hill on this very sensitive subject. Those White House guys were playing a good game of poker. Their cards were close to their vests, and their mouths were shut. And they hated leaks to the press! So why should he risk taking the flak for an unexplained leak?

No, that wouldn't be worth it! But maybe there was another way to play this one. *Maybe,* he thought, *I can kill two birds with one stone. Maybe I could feed Bryce's name to Justice, and they could squeeze him under FISA and Patriot Act. Section 1801-e,2,B of FISA might do it. It justified surveillance on the grounds that the government needed the information in order to properly conduct foreign policy. After all, Bryce was really trying to influence American foreign policy by obtaining, or trying to obtain, classified information about the administration's intention to go to war preemptively against Razik. That information could affect our foreign policy against Razik. That would certainly be a secu-*

rity problem, wouldn't it, and FISA was all about national security, wasn't it?

Yes, a newspaperman trying to steal classified information, that's it! If he could nail this squealer, maybe the White House would appreciate it enough to provide the intelligence committee with some solid information about what they were actually going to do to Razik. And his boss, the congressman from Wyoming, definitely appreciated someone like that who could think outside the box, particularly where it paid off with some good, hard information later for the committee. Yes, he had the way to play this one.

As soon as Reinwater got back to his office, he picked up his phone and called the Washington office of the FBI. "Agent Jelski is in, and he'll be glad to take your call," the receptionist said in professional manner.

"Yes," Jelski responded after picking up the call. "I can take some information down and refer it to the internal security office."

"No, I cannot take <u>that</u> kind of information over the phone. It either has to be in writing or you'll have to stop in personally and file the complaint." Jelski replied.

"Doesn't the bureau want to get tips?" Reinwater questioned.

"Yes, they do, but there are procedures that have to be followed—important procedures needed to assure the reliability and credibility of the information being offered to the FBI."

"For instance?"

"For instance, how am I supposed to know who I am talking to? How can I confirm that you are the person you say you are? For all I know, Reinwater could be Santa Claus in disguise," Jelski concluded.

Reinwater, who had been with the Intelligence Committee on Capitol Hill for over five years, and was thoroughly acquainted with working procedures, said, "Are you some kind of rulemonger, or do you just like to be a nitpicker?"

Jelski then shot back, "You know, I don't make these rules. Most of them are based on compliance with something called the Federal Rules of Evidence, which were created in a place called Congress. Ever heard of it? I just follow those rules, so I can sleep at night. And oh, by the way, my wife likes me to bring home a regular paycheck at the end of each week. You do understand that, don't you, sir?"

Undeterred, Reinwater continued, "Well, a reporter is trying to obtain classified information on what our country is planning to do in Razik, and what we do in Razik is part of this country's foreign policy. If he gets the information that he is after, and publishes it, that would most certainly affect the foreign policy of this country. So you should be able to get the FISA court to grant a surveillance order under 50 U.S. Code subd. (e), (2), B shouldn't you? Why don't you give that a try? That would be information our country needs to conduct our foreign policy. That constitutes 'foreign intelligence' information and would be covered by FISA. We need to have this reporter on the radar screen."

Jelski replied that he understood he was talking to an employee of the Congressional Intelligence Committee, and that the committee had oversight over some aspects of the FBI's work, and that Reinwater also knew what he was talking about. But that didn't change the FBI's policy relating to the credibility of the informant's tip. Yes, he could take the name of the newspaper reporter, along with Reinwater's name, and write up the complaint, but Jake would still have to come in the next morning and swear to its accuracy. At that point Jelski could then turn over the complaint to Foreign Intelligence and suggest that they put Bryce on the "screen" if they could find him in Washington.

But even as he said this to Reinwater, he had to chuckle to himself. Even that congressional bird-dog had acted tentative about whether they could fit Bryce in under the definition of foreign intelligence. But, in fact, Jelski knew that if he wrote it up in the proper format for a legal application to the FISA court, it would be approved. Although over ten thousand "ex-parte" applications had been made to the secret FISA court in the first ten years of the court's existence, none of them had ever been denied. It was like the running back on a football team trying to score a touchdown against a team that had no defenders on the field. Since the application would be made to the court on a *ex parte* basis, nobody would appear in opposition to the request, so there would be nobody to challenge the accuracy of the facts alleged in the petition, or to argue that there weren't grounds for granting the application. Further, under the law, the judges had no authority to use their own discretion in deciding whether to approve an order. THEY BASICALLY HAD TO APPROVE IT IF NOBODY PRESENTED ANY EVIDENCE CHALLENGING THE EVIDENCE OFFERED BY THE EXECUTIVE DEPARTMENT. So, by default, they had to approve the request! What a farce! Best of all, since the court's order was a secret, nobody else would ever see it, so it certainly wouldn't be challenged later for insufficiency in law or fact.

Ultimately, though, in 98 percent of these prior investigations, Jelski knew, there never was sufficient evidence found to obtain any criminal conviction. *Startling really,* Jelski thought to himself. *Why were 98 percent of the cases necessary in the first place?*

The next day, after Reinwater appeared in the office to

sign the complaint, Jelski was immediately on the phone to Silovich in the National Security Office. Jelski told him this was some "pain in the butt" who worked for the House Intelligence Committee who had filed a complaint against some newspaper reporter out of New York City who was snooping around for classified information on Capitol Hill. "Yes," he said in answer to Silovich's question, "the reporter was asking about whether the Administration intended to go to war over the weapons of mass destruction that Razik was alleged to have. Yes," Jelski elaborated further, "the tipster was familiar with FISA because of his employment with the Intelligence Committee, and he thought the Foreign Counter-Intelligence Department should try to get an order to put the reporter on the 'screen.' Yes, the 'radar screen.' Yes," Jelski added, "Reinwater's social security number did check out," and Jelski did remember talking to him before. "Reporter's name? Bryce—John Bryce."

Then, after listening to Silovich for a minute, Jelski said, "Oh, tell the Intelligence Committee guy to stop worrying. He's two steps behind you guys? You've already got Bryce on radar. You got a tip from the Pentagon earlier that he was nosing around over there too? So he's already on the screen, when you can catch him, that is! Okay, I'll let Reinwater know. Yes, of course, certainly, that will be off the record. Definitely, yes, good-bye."

X

Bryce Throws Out a Line at Foggy Bottom

John Bryce was beginning to feel confused. He worked for a great newspaper that had a long history of service to the Republic. And now the American Republic appeared to be readying itself to go to war in the Middle East. Yet nobody in Washington knew for sure whether the U.S. would invade. Alternatively, if they did know what was going to happen, they wouldn't talk with his newspaper about it. He couldn't figure out why there was such a void of information available to him on such an important subject.

Although the U.N. inspection in Razik had been conducted vigorously and at random throughout Razik, the results were still inconclusive—no caches of poison gas, activated uranium that could be used in nuclear bombs, nor biological agents had actually been found. Certainly, no nuclear weapons or plants that could build them had been found.

So what was America going to do in this situation? Would they support further inspections, or did they plan to go to war anyway, notwithstanding this inconclusive evidence? Why couldn't Bryce find someone to confirm what was going on? Had the newspaper's friends in Washington abandoned them? Why couldn't he dig up any information about the planning being done within the Administration for the next step to be taken? Perhaps an old classmate who had been working for the State Department in Washington at the time of his last college reunion could clarify some of those questions. A quick check of the class website confirmed that Judy Dimpreo was in fact still employed in Washington at Foggy Bottom. Not wanting to disturb her at work, he elected to call her at home at 7:30 P.M., hopefully shortly after she had returned from work.

Judy Dimpreo was still her old vivacious self, and she indicated that she was pleased to hear from her old Psi U fraternity brother. Their college was one of the few in the country that had experimented with allowing young women to join fraternities. She had been one of the first brave young college girls to opt to try fraternity life, although she had never actually lived in the fraternity house with the other Psi U Rams.

Thus it was no surprise to Bryce that Judy invited him over to her apartment, nor that she gave him the old fraternity handshake, with the respective second and little fingers crossing over each other, when he arrived at the door. But he quickly dispelled any notion that he was there for fun and games. He told her that he was a married man, and, in fact, had married the same girl that he had dated in college and whom Judy had already met at college fraternity parties. And he also told her why he was in Washington, and of the urgency of his mission for the *Times*.

Turning down a glass of Dewer's White Label Scotch, he settled for a glass of California Chardonnay which Judy poured for him as he pleaded his case for some information about the intentions of the U.S. government with respect to Razik. After listening to John Bryce while pouring the two glasses of Chardonnay, she sat down on the couch on the opposite side of the room from John, turned somber and paused, and then started to respond slowly to the question.

Choosing her words carefully, she said, "Well, frankly it is not surprising to me that you are asking all these questions, because many of us at Foggy Bottom have been asking the very same questions for the past three months. We go to our meetings here at the State Department. We itemize the problems that we think the U.S. will have to face if they invade Razik. We mention what happened when the U.S. propped up the Shah of Iran in the 1950s in order to stabilize that oil-rich region—and then how the Shah was later overthrown by the Fundamentalist Moslem Revolution. The American embassy was attacked and surrounded, the Americans were then held hostage in Iran in 1981, and finally America was denounced and thrown out of Iran. Then we file our reports and make our recommendations to our superiors—and that is the last we hear of them.

"Frankly," she continued, "almost no one that I know at State is in favor of attacking Razik. But we have also concluded that we are just not on the president's team at State. Furthermore, we are apparently completely out of the loop, and thus we don't hear anything about the administration's plans and don't know what they have in mind for the future. In fact, we don't even know what they have in mind for next week!

"So, sad to tell, that is my story," she concluded. As John Bryce studied her expressions and listened to her frustrated voice—a voice he knew from many long discussions carried on at the "armpit" back at the House only ten or twelve years ago—he finally understood. He could communicate easily with Judy and with others he had talked to in Washington. But nobody that he could talk with could tell him anything that he could use for his story for the *Times*—because those people in Washington didn't know anything about the country's plans for Razik in the first place. They were also on the "outs" in Washington—left out of the loop of information that perhaps was traveling around Washington. For all the communicating they did, the new Administration might just as well have spoken a foreign language.

As he left Judy's apartment after having a further discussion with her about which fraternity members were living and working where, he thought about giving her the old fraternity slap on the backside, but instead decided that would no longer be in keeping with his professional station in life. So instead, he just thanked her for inviting him over, and for the drink, and explaining what she knew about Razik. He also promised to buy her a drink at the next reunion.

XI
Getting Back to Jill

Karl Erskine had not forgotten that last date with Jill. He thought about it every day. It really bothered him. Everything had seemed to go well all that evening. But it still crashed at the end. He couldn't understand what happened. Things like that really bothered him. First she seemed to like him, then she didn't. Why?

He decided he had to do something about it; so he called her again. Would she like to go for a ride to Rehobeth Beach this Saturday? He said he would really like to talk to her. She would? Great! Yes, he would be there at 9:30 A.M. to pick her up.

He got there in his usual punctual manner the following Saturday. It was a bright summer's day, with a temperature of about 82 degrees. As they drove along Route 404 eastward to the coast of Maryland, they chatted easily about a number of things, including the weather, work, vacation plans, and how they felt. So he finally decided to take a conversational chance, and ask her about the screwy thing she did at the end of their last date. "Oh that," she replied, as she twisted abruptly in the passenger's seat so that she was looking away from him. "Do you really want me to get into that again? Just when we are enjoying ourselves again?" Since he couldn't think of anything that sounded right, he just continued to think and said nothing.

After a long pause, she finally broke the silence and said sadly, "Well, if you do something silly, I guess you have to be prepared to explain it later." She sounded somewhat embarrassed. "Well, what happened is something like this. I was a little depressed from work before you picked me up on our last date. Then I felt a lot better as we got talking and had a good dinner. Then you started to talk about your new job, and your promotion, and the fact that everything was secret. Then I started looking down into that dark old bar, and read on the sign about the slaves being kept in a dungeon there before the Civil War. And I thought about how slavery had actually been accepted in half the country before it was finally defeated.

"Then I started thinking about all the newspaper articles and letters to the editor saying that the government was taking away our civil liberties in order to fight terrorism. Then you started to talk about the fact that you were fighting terrorism, and that your work was all classified and you couldn't talk about it anymore. Then I thought about my father who was in the Army in World War II and fought in Germany, and the way he was always upset every time he saw pictures of the new American Army helmets that came out in the early 1980s. He always used to say, 'Those damned Army helmets always remind me of the Nazi helmets in World War II. The British and the Israelis have modern helmets too, but they don't look like ours. What are they trying to do—re-write history visually? I suppose people will look at the pictures in a few years and actually think that the Nazis won World War II!'

"So then, on the way home," she continued, "I began to wonder if the reason you couldn't tell me anything about your work was that you were involved in taking away people's rights. And I began to wonder what was happening to our civil liberties? And I wanted to ask you what you thought was happening, but I decided I couldn't. So that made me depressed again, and I decided I did not want to go out with you again. So then I gave you the 'Heil' sign to let you know what I was thinking—so you would understand." She then sat silently in the car, looking the other way, and quietly wiped a tear from the corner of her left eye.

Never lacking in perception, Karl immediately understood what had happened. "Now I completely understand the problem. In fact, I know exactly how you felt, because that's the way I felt while listening to the orientation lecture given to us at the office the other day. In fact, we were told that everything about the job and the lecture were classified and we couldn't talk about it to anyone.

"But that doesn't really solve the problem, does it?" he murmured half to himself and half to Jill. Then they both went into a long period of silence, when it was a lot easier to just watch the fields of corn and wheat go by and disappear back into the rearview mirrors. So they dropped the subject, and just did their best to enjoy a pleasant day at Rehobeth Beach on the coast of Delaware.

XII

Erskine Goes into the Foreign Counter-Intelligence Tunnel: "Everything Is Perfectly Legal"

On Karl Erskine's next trip to the Audio-Visual Room of the Foreign Counter-Intelligence Office, he was less than enthusiastic about going in. He didn't have all of the answers about what was involved in his work, but he was beginning to suspect that this job might not turn out to be the All-American assignment he had been hoping to get.

The schedule for today called for a lecture on the current state of the law pertaining to Foreign Intelligence. As he sat down, he noticed that the podium that had been used the other day by Sam Silovich was once again back at the front of the room. Except this time, he noticed, with a sigh of relief, the lecturer, who was already behind the podium, was a lot better looking. A woman, no less. Apparently a female attorney was going to brief them on the clandestine subject of Foreign Intelligence, or more precisely, Foreign Counter-Intelligence.

She introduced herself as Shirley Bethour. She mentioned that she had been at the Justice Department for six years after graduating from Yale Law School. As she got further into her subject, she apparently felt secure enough to move further and further away from the podium, alternately going from one side to the other. As she did so, Karl got a chance to evaluate her appearance. Her attire was professional enough, but she had not lost her femininity. As she droned on about FISA—the Foreign Intelligence Surveillance Act—and section 2511 of 18, USCA—her movements made her lecture somewhat more interesting.

Aside from the loose-fitting cardigan sweater, she wore a neatly pleated gray skirt—more typical of the bobby-sock era of way back—which rubbed back and forth over her textured black stockings, which in turn featured the curving lines of her legs every time she moved. And every time she had an important point to make, she emphasized it with a wide swing of her hips, as she typically moved back in the opposite direction, causing her skirt to swing back and forth, like a lantern from a post. With that action, Karl perceived that this dry subject might be more interesting than he had anticipated.

Perhaps detecting his eye movements, Shirley remonstrated dryly, "For those of you who are up to this subject, I will try to bring you up to date on the law of foreign intelligence surveillance as it stands today."

Well, thought Karl, *at least someone was being frank about what they were doing in this unit; conducting clandestine surveillance on various foreign spies.* So they must have been looking at videos—apparently secretly taken—on unwitting spies or suspects. The severe warning on the door of the Audio-Visual Room was designed to keep this new type of surveillance a secret, and apparently had been successful in doing just that, since he had never heard of anything like this before.

"The name on the door of this room is 'Audio-Visual,' " Shirley Bethour continued. "And when you first started your training in this unit, you started working with tapes having only video surveillance—no sound. There are reasons for that. These two subjects—audio and visual surveillance—are treated differently under the law. The key is that there are currently almost no legal limitations on visual videotaping or surveillance, either under federal law or the law of most states. There are generally no statutes that prohibit videotaping on private property if there is no sound being recorded, except for a few states that prohibit videotaping on private property (as a violation of the right of privacy). But these state statutes are pre-empted by federal statutes dealing with national security and terrorism. Absent that, there are no federal statutes which prohibit videotaping.

"With respect to videotaping in private places, there are no federal court decisions prohibiting that activity either. Specifically, the ninth Circuit Court of Appeals held in *U.S. v. Koyomejian* in 1992 that neither the Foreign Intelligence Surveillance Act or Title I, nor the wiretapping statue, regulates silent, domestic video surveillance undertaken as part of a criminal investigation if done pursuant to a court order. Neither are there any cases decided under the FISA Act that say that the person or persons subject to that surveillance must ever be notified of that fact. So the subject is never supposed to be aware of this surveillance by a camera right in the home or office. The exception is where the subject is later prosecuted and evidence from FISA tapes is offered as evidence at a criminal trial.

Kyllo v. U.S. the United States Supreme Court decision written by Justice Scalia, involved the use by Federal agents, without a court order, of thermography equipment, designed to measure heat emanating from the house, outside a suspect's house. The equipment was of course being used to determine if excessive heat was being emitted from the suspect's house. The purpose was to find out if artificial light was being used to grow marijuana inside the house. In that case, Justice Scalia held that the homeowner should not be left to the mercy of advanced investigative technology. Justice Scalia stated that, 'in the sanctity of the home, all details are intimate details.'

"But *Kyllo* can be distinguished from this process that we use in this office, because here we are videotaping the inside of people's homes, whereas in *Kyllo,* the thermograph devices were being used outside the home to measure heat outside the home. Thus the facts are different.

"Another reason why we are not governed by the *Kyllo* decision, or—in legal language, why we are not bound by the *Kyllo* precedent in this office—is that we first obtain a FISA court order, before we do our videotaping in people's houses using our new, secret methodology for taping what goes on inside people's homes. So we are legal because we have, or get, a court order in every case that we need one.

"And even if we did not have a court order in a few emergency cases, we are of the opinion that the dicta in *Kyllo* regarding homeowners not being at 'the mercy of advancing technology' has no application here, because, as I have mentioned, of the different facts that we have here—the cases are thus distinguishable. There is no law that I know of that says how far out our dicta applies, or whether dicta has to be respected or given effect in any event. We see no necessity of speculating as to how far out—to how many different sets of facts—the court would apply the principle of 'sanctity' of the home set forth in *Kyllo.* We deal with the present here, not the past, or the precedents from the past. And for the present, there is definitely no precedent that prevents the type of surveillance that we are currently undertaking in this unit.

"Under the Patriot Act, and with the FISA court available to us, the Executive Department makes the law, not the judiciary anymore, because, under FISA THE JUDGES HAVE TO DO WHAT WE TELL THEM TO DO. So we do not have to establish probable cause anymore, or prove that there is probable cause to believe that a crime has been committed before we can commence surveillance. For instance, formerly we could never get surveillance on an honest and loyal American who would never consider breaking the law. Now we can do just that, if the information we seek is necessary for a pre-existing FBI investigation already underway, or if we feel it is necessary to the national defense or to conduct American foreign policy.

"So, obviously we could obtain surveillance on anybody in this room if we want, whether you continue in this program or drop out. So be sure to pay your respects to me on the way out at the end of the lecture." She paused at this point, apparently hoping for laughter, but was disappointed.

"As you can see, if we allege that some person is in possession of information or data that is necessary to our state security in some way, we exercise very broad powers. For example, if someone traveled to Mexico or France they might obtain or learn something that our government might need to know in order to reassess its policies toward that country. And so that is the type of information that you will be looking for in your security tape analysis.

"Furthermore, since no court has ever held that FISA is unconstitutional, we are justified in assuming that it is constitutional in every respect. The fact that there *have* been so *few* challenges to its constitutionality in the courts makes constitutionality irrelevant as a practical matter. Arguably the statute was designed in the first place by Congress to be free of legal challenges. For instance, ninety-eight percent of the persons who are subject to surveillance orders never find out that surveillance has taken place, because they are never notified of that fact by the government. Obviously, if you never know that the government is conducting surveillance, and there is no way you can find out about it even if you try, then there is no way you can challenge the legality of that which you are unaware of in the first place. So perhaps we should not worry too much about constitutionality here anyway.

"Thus the FISA Statute and the Patriot Act, in effect, amend the Fourth Amendment to the Constitution by eliminating the requirement that 'no warrants shall issue, but upon probable cause,' as well as by ignoring the principle stated in the Fourth Amendment that 'The right of the people to be secure in their persons, houses, papers, and effects, against unreasonable searches and seizures, shall not be violated.' FISA essentially eliminates the Fourth Amendment standard for searches or intrusions into the home and replaces it with a standard of 'government need to know.'

"Pretty clever, isn't it? Nobody can bring a case against the government to challenge the legality of surveillance because they never find out about it in the first place. And if no case or controversy is ever brought before the court, then the overall constitutionality of FISA is NEVER TESTED IN THE FIRST PLACE. Possibly as a result of this the Supreme Court has never passed on the constitutionality of FISA up to this time.

"Now please don't ask me," Shirley Bethour continued peremptorily, "if Congress had enacted an unconstitutional statute here, which by its nature cannot be challenged in our court system. Hey, my job here isn't to give legal advice to the opposition, is it?

"Now if I seem overly expansive here, that is because we are in a bind. When this stuff is sent to us, we have no choice but to do it, like it or not. And it can be very frustrating and demoralizing!

"Remember, Congress has spoken on this subject. I may or may not agree with some part of this statute—even though there is no doubt that its main purpose to combat terrorism is absolutely legitimate—that doesn't mean that I agree with all of these provisions. And if you can figure a way out of these constitutional puzzles, be my guest!

"How do you rationalize our need to investigate dangerous foreign spies and terrorists with the right of the American public to be protected from unreasonable searches of their homes, as protected by the Constitution?

"But doing the thinking of the opposition isn't my job, is it?" she continued, suddenly red-faced and flustered by her quick reactions to her own talk. "Well, listen, I'm still a human being, aren't I? Remember, I still have to be able to go to sleep at night too. And since I can't discuss any of these subjects with the folks I live with, because it is all classified and confidential, our guidelines tell us to get everything off our chests at work. So that's what I'm doing. This way I can get these nagging questions off my mind and get back to work sooner.

"Not only that, it is my responsibility to tell you," she continued with renewed concentration, "that the public is not yet ready to be told what we are doing here. And I don't need to remind you this is classified information, and it is my job and yours to make sure it stays that way. So you are compelled by law to keep all of this, including my off-the-cuff remarks to you a moment ago, under the hat.

"So much for the visual element of videotaping in the home, and for the reasons why neither the wire-tapping laws, nor FISA, nor the Supreme Court decision in *U.S. v. Kyllo* involving the 'sanctity of the home' principle, prohibits or prevents our work here.

"Now, with respect to capturing the suspect's voice on videotape, surprisingly, that is treated entirely differently under existing law. The interception of the subject's voice on the videotape itself does fall under the federal wiretap laws, specifically under 18 USC, section 2501 and thereafter. Picking up a voice, even on a videotape, is a prohibited interception under the wiretapping statute, unless we first obtain a court order from a federal court. But if we do go to the FISA court with our request for that order, we only need to prove, in the case of an American citizen, that the government needs information about that person in order to properly conduct our foreign policy. Before FISA and the Patriot Act we would have had to prove that there was probable cause to believe a crime had been committed in order to get surveillance. But now all we have to prove is, essentially, government 'need to know.' So the emphasis has switched from protecting the individual to protecting the state—the security of the state, the United States—is now paramount. But once we have the court order, we can use the voice element as well as the picture itself.

"Since we are now using both the picture and the voice, you may now possibly be concerned that we are seeing or hearing things in people's homes that we shouldn't be, like sex or nudity, for instance. But you can relax on that score as well. The FSA statute, revolutionary as it is, has a solution to that problem as well. Under 50 USC section 1806, there is a provision requiring the destruction of unintentionally acquired information. So we create our own privacy screen. It enables us to edit any and all offensive materials from our tapes. Later on, in fact, you may be requested to help us edit our pornographic material from videotapes.

"Now I can tell you that FISA and the Patriot Act give us a more efficient way of gathering evidence than we had previously. As far as we are concerned, FISA evidence trumps ordinary evidence because it is easier to get in the first place and remains hidden from the opponent's view longer. With this new way to gather evidence we, of course, become the stars of the show. Like Eliot Ness, we always get our man.

"So if that isn't a grand slam for the executive branch of government and law enforcement, I don't know what is. It's like legislative branch gave the winning lottery ticket to the executive branch of government. What a giveaway! Do you know, Congress doesn't even conduct any hearing to see how FISA is working out?

"So we may conclude, I believe, in light of the latitude that Congress is giving us on FISA matter—I don't know if they are giving us enough rope to hang ourselves with, or they just want to watch human nature really play out—that Congress has now created a much stronger executive branch than this country has had in the past fifty years. Congress has, in fact, apparently divested itself of some of its power, although ostensibly that is only in the area of foreign counterintelligence. Not only is it stepping away from acting as a check on the actions of the executive department, but it has also effectively hobbled the judicial branch of government by depriving them of their usual right of judicial review over the actions of the FISA court, as well as their usual right to review the constitutionality of the FISA statute itself. For instance, after twenty-seven years, the Supreme Court hasn't had a chance to decide whether the FISA court itself is constitutional.

"The geniuses who wrote these statutes effectively amended, in de facto fashion, the First, Fourth, Fifth, and Sixth Amendments to the U.S. Constitution, and created a secret court whose decisions are never made part of the public record and whose decisions can never be read by the public or even by the affected defendant. It is really an alternative legal system that by-passes the constitutionally based federal court system. It is bound by different rules of evidence, procedure, and even has its own appeals court. Frankly, not even the Star Chamber ever had it so good! The ship of state has thus been redesigned and re-tooled for the twenty-first century, even though most people in this country are totally unaware of it. Too bad, really!

"So, on paper here, it's not like Congress doesn't know what is going on here. We are only doing what we are told to do and what has been approved by the legislative branch. Congress even has the right under FISA to repeal or modify the statute, but has never made any fundamental changes. So they approve of what we are doing. Basically, they are making it easy for the good guys—the government guys—to catch the bad Americans, even if it is with their pants down." When she had to pause to allow the raucous laughter to calm down, she realized that she was finally making progress.

At this point, Roger Kaiser, who was sitting in the back of the room, stood up and said abruptly, "All right, Shirley, I think we have gone far enough here today, particularly since you seem to be wearing down here. So let's end it for today."

XIII
Bringing Karl in for a Soft Landing

Ever alert to his new recruit's reaction to events, Roger then turned toward Karl Erskine. He immediately perceived that Karl seemed to be fully absorbed in his own thoughts. Thinking he might still be able to help Karl get started on his new job with a soft landing, Roger inquired, "Karl, any interest in a cup of coffee down at the cafeteria?"

Somewhat startled at being caught unawares, Karl could not think of any reason not to join Roger for coffee, and replied, "Sure, why not?"

As they headed down the hallway to the elevator, Roger lamented, "Boy, Shirley really lost it! That's the problem with the really bright legal-eagles. They get upset if everything isn't just right. They get all bent out of shape if we don't do things here the way they used to in their Nancy Drew books. But what are we going to do? We need their brains at this point, so I guess we just have to keep them in pampers, which is certainly appropriate for some of them.

"But," Roger continued, "on the other hand, I did think she did a good job of indirectly explaining the 'electric fence' as we call it. First the electronic wiretap to get at the phone communications, then the sneak and peak plumber's entry while the owners are away, and then the secret taped surveillance in the home. Still, she seems to be hung up on this idea of 'fairness.' Hey, we all know that went out the window on 9/11, right?"

Somewhat surprised that he was still part of Roger's conversational orbit, Karl was once again caught off guard. So he made a bogus donation to the conversation. "Yeah, she was both very perceptive in her legal analysis, and somewhat childish at the same time. Maybe she was ill-at-ease with the subject matter."

Boy, what an understatement, he thought immediately as he said it. She had seemed as though she was almost ready to puke at some of that stuff she had to say. Simultaneously he made a mental note that his intuitive observation about their lecturer would be on a wavelength that Roger was not going to pick up in any event.

As they got on the elevator and went down to the next floor to the cafeteria, Roger seemed to be thinking further about his supervisory responsibilities. He seemed to be reviewing in his own mind the lecture just finished by Shirley, perhaps analyzing it for further strengths and weaknesses.

After they both got their coffee, cream and sugar and settled in at an open table, he picked up where he had left off. "On balance, though, I thought she did a good job. The main point that had to be made was that the procedures we are using here are perfectly legal! They have all been approved in a law, the foreign Intelligence Surveillance Act, that was passed by Congress a long time ago. And now the Patriot Act has really ratified the things we were doing all along.

"You know," Roger continued, "they really did a sweet job on drafting those statutes. They are really innovative. Do you know there is even a provision in them that permits the government to go to a cable or satellite television company and demand that they turn over all the information relating to the target's account? They have to give us the target's access code—the code that identifies the RF signals being given off spontaneously by the television set—which permits us to view their home through the camera secreted in the black box or the TV itself, as the case may be. We can even get access through a 'sneak and peak' and add our equipment to an old TV if need be. Can you beat that for ingenuity?"

Karl Erskine once again merely nodded his assent. He had already concluded from the unfocused look in Roger's eyes that was all that was necessary. His boss really wasn't looking for any input from him any longer. His subconscious appeared to have won. Just any listening post would do. After they finished their coffee and chat, Roger appeared to feel more relaxed. Having apparently concluded the day's business to his satisfaction, he started to look ahead. "Could you set aside some time in a couple of days to get some training on the editing of tapes?" he asked. Karl duly agreed to that request, bade Roger adieu, and returned to his office.

XIV
Bryce Reports Back to the Paper

Time was once again closing in on John Bryce. He had been in Washington another full week, and was scheduled to meet with the Washington editor at his office today. Yet as he drove down Eleventh Street toward the paper's office, he kept asking himself how he could explain to the *Times* staff that he had been unable to document a story.

As he was thinking, a SUV coming from the opposite direction suddenly swerved over the center line toward his car. Then, just as suddenly, the SUV swerved back away from his car. Not more than thirty seconds later, as he once again tried to put together a possible storyline to lay out to the newspaper, another oncoming car suddenly swung over toward him. This time he noticed the driver, who appeared to be a young man in his early twenties. *These kids certainly don't know how to drive,* he thought, as he went the last few blocks to the *Times* office.

As he went, he tried to put together his thoughts. Despite his strenuous efforts, he had been unable to dig up any information about the president's intentions to go to war, one way or the other. If the United Nations Security Council refused to authorize an attack on Razik, nobody seemed to know what the U.S. planned to do.

He had probably put that very question to at least fifty knowledgeable people in the District of Columbia so far.

But there had been two different points of view in the answers he got. The first was that the U.S. had sounded tough all along, as if it had made up its mind, in order to pressure Razik into complying with a prior U.S. Resolution directing Razik to disarm and permit further U.N. inspections.

The other answer that he had gotten was that President Muller had, in fact, already made up his mind a long time ago based on terrorist events that had taken place over many years, and was going to try to take the heart out of terrorism, right in Razik. The absence of any proof that Razik had participated in any prior terrorist attacks against the U.S. was considered by the Administration to be simply "reality based analysis" which did not impact their reasoning.

So the story was, he felt, that either no decision had yet been made by the U.S., or that if it had been, nobody was willing to take the considerable risk involved in leaking that information to the press, to someone like John Bryce.

As he walked up the stairway to the *Times'* Washington office, he felt reasonably confident that he could sell the editor on the correctness of his general conclusions. But he also had a few qualms that the brass might instead conclude that he could not cut the mustard as a reporter in the nation's capitol. Overall, though, he still felt confident that he had analyzed the situation correctly. If he could convince the Washington staff, then he could bang out a three-part article explaining how he came to his conclusions. He could point out that senior Administration officials seemed to be enjoying bringing the American electorate, and world opinion, into a raging debate on what could, or should, be done in Razik. Like good actors, the Administration was artfully building suspense to a crescendo before springing the surprise climax on this audience. By now, millions around the world were being brought into the debate.

But, even though he had no hard evidence to prove it, John Bryce had concluded that President Muller had already decided that he would attack Razik now, before it had the opportunity to use its weapons of mass destruction on this country. Otherwise, why had the president called up thousands of reservists and members of the National Guard? Would an astute politician like the president spend millions of dollars to send two hundred thousands troops to the Persian Gulf and then back down? John felt that was not only unlikely, but highly improbable. The "hawks" would not back down. If they did, it would not sit well with the voters at the next election. Bryce felt the public had been persuaded that an attack was necessary. They had been prepared for an attack by the president's firm and consistent manner on Razik. As a result, the president probably felt that they would be pleased to re-elect a successful hawk.

With all that in mind, John strode into the paper's second floor conference room, where Charles Ball and Dwight Percival, the military correspondent and legal counsel, respectively, were once again waiting for him with the Washington editor. After an exchange of initial pleasantries, Bryce got right to the point. "Gentlemen, I don't have a precise answer to the question assigned to me. But, analytically, and based on anecdotal conversations I've had here, there are two possibilities. The first is that the Administration will not make up its mind on Razik until after we have gone to the U.N. for another vote of approval.

"The other possibility is that a decision has been made, but very few people know what it is. And those that do, will not reveal it. Two things point in the latter direction.

"First, the president has already announced his new policy of pre-emptive strike against possible future military opponents who might be pre-disposed to attack the U.S. later with weapons of mass destruction. Although Razik has never attacked the U.S., there is no doubt that they are very critical of U.S. foreign policy in the Middle East. They have also used weapons like poison gas before. Thus, who can say that Raznik might not attack the U.S. in the future in the same manner?

"Second, the movement of U.S. troops to the Persian Gulf tends to support the conclusion that President Muller, a smart politician, has already made up his mind. Would he go through all the dislodgement of reservists from private jobs without actually using them? I don't believe so. By exercising the broad discretion already given him by Congress, he intends to go to war whether or not the U.N. Security Council approves. If they don't approve, then our own national security still comes first, and we will invade Razik anyway.

"The problem, of course, is how do we prove that? Unfortunately, I have not found any Daniel Ellsberg willing to give us a package of secret papers that I could base my story on. I suppose you could just let me loose with a by-line and let me lay out the same analysis that I have just given to you. But I just didn't know what you would decide, so I haven't written anything up to now. I have spent all my time interviewing people, trying to locate some documentary or conclusive proof. I'm sorry, but you'll have to tell me where to go from here."

XV
Cleaning Up the Tapes

Karl Erskine was back at work on the surveillance tapes in the Office of National Security. This time he was there for a lesson on the editing of surveillance tapes. It was like using the vacuum cleaner, he was told. Just clean up the dirt.

Shirley Bethour, the legal-eagle who had given them the lecture earlier, was back for a curtain call on the basics of cleaning up the tapes, so that they could be used in the developing legal process at a later time, if necessary.

"What we want to do here," she began "is to sanitize these tapes so that they can be sent into the offices of federal district court judges around the country, to be used to oppose discovery requests, motions in limine before trial and all bail hearings and the like. Generally these tapes will be reviewed 'in camera,' which means in private, by the judge and will not be seen by the defendant's attorneys. Nevertheless, they will be seen by the Judge's law clerks and possibly occasionally by secretaries. Obviously we don't want to shoot our reputations in the foot before we start. So we cannot have these tapes filled with pictures of our nude subjects, or a target in bed with someone with an ulterior motive. So we clean these tapes up before they leave this office. We also don't want any of our own employees seeing some of the outrageous stuff that we pick up during surveillance before it leaves here. Therefore we meticulously edit out anything that could be seen by anyone to be pornographic. The equipment that we use to do this consists of a VCR, a copier, and the erase button on the VCR.

"If we come onto anything pornographic in reviewing the tapes, we then isolate the beginning and end of the pornographic scene. We then run off a copy of that portion, mark it for identification and place it in the trash file for preservation. That done, we then reattach the tape again and rerun it to make sure that we got out all the pornographic material.

"Now obviously, the difficult part of this is determining what is actually offensively pornographic. 'PG-13' stuff is okay at the movies and it is also okay in our surveillance tapes. 'X-rated' stuff, however, is definitely taboo on our tapes and has to be edited out. Now for anything in between those two ratings, such as partial nudity, we apply the established legal test of knowing it when we see it.

"So, with that in mind, you can now start editing your sample tape. Incidentally, the reason we have to preserve copies of the porno material is to permit our supervisors to determine if we are doing our jobs correctly. Before you start on your tape, though, I want you to get your emotions under control. Unfortunately, we've learned from this work that quite a few people choose to go around the home as 'scantily clads.' "

Karl Erskine, whose family had always been scrupulous about such types of things, felt as though the other shoe had dropped. He was shocked that the government had gotten into such prying, but he knew there was absolutely nothing that he could do about it. Resignedly, he started to load his tape into the VCR.

The particular tape that had been assigned to him had apparently been left unmarked and unidentified, so the identity of the persons being videotaped on it were also unknown to him. As it came up on the screen, the image once again showed the inside of a suburban-type house. A woman was sitting on a couch, looking right into the camera at perhaps a distance of fifteen feet. The sound of a male newscaster could clearly be heard reciting the national news for the morning. As Karl studied the tape, he gathered he was supposed to determine whether the woman's negligee left her sufficiently exposed so that the scene had to be deleted. Queasily he started to examine the details, but was suddenly interrupted as the door in the back of the room burst open and Sam Silovich rushed in, speaking in an excited tone as he came.

"Shut down your tapes, folks. We've an incoming real-time event that you can pick you on your monitors if you hit the 'real-time' icon. We're picking up, if you can believe it, a conference at the office of the *Washington Times* paper. There must be some kind of wireless camera in there, because one of our agents picked it up by accident. We don't have an order on this one, so it must be some kind of private, random snooping going on. I believe the camera that's picking this up is in the editor's office."

As Erskine's monitor lit up with the new picture, Silovich studied it for a moment, and then said quickly, "See that white-haired guy at the end of the conference table there. That's the Washington editor of the *Times.* I recognize him from newspaper pictures. He's apparently watching the midday news with a couple of his staff people. And that guy just coming into the room and sitting down is Charlie Ball, their military reporter. If you can goose up the audio there, we may be able to find out what this conference is going to be about."

As the sound turned up, the voice of a newscaster could be clearly heard, "Today's events in Razik seem to be getting tenser by the hour. Frankly, it looks as though the country is preparing for an American attack." At that point the two men at the conference table then leaned forward, as if to hear the rest of the newscast better. Then, as the voice of the newscaster seemed to fade, you could then hear the discussion between the two newspapermen. The younger man, Charlie Ball, was speaking, "The bottom line on our story about the possible invasion of Razik is that Bryce does not have anything definite. He just doesn't have any hard facts to base a story on. But he does make a good case, I feel, that the Administration is going to do something soon. He feels that the call-up of the reserves and National Guard and the plans to send troops to the Middle East definitely means that the U.S. plans to go to war, and soon. I think we should let him go ahead and write up his analysis; that's the best and only story that we've got."

Just at that moment, the door of the Audio-Visual room, where all eyes were glued to the drama unfolding at the *Times,* banged open again. This time it was Shirley Bethour who stormed in holding a newspaper in her right hand above her head. "Guys, I just picked this up on Pennsylvania Avenue during lunch hour. Will you look at this headline!" Across the top of the front page of the Washington Eagle News was a headline in large, two-inch-high letters: "U.S. PLANES HIT RAZIK PREEMPTIVELY IN EARLY MORNING RAID TODAY." The next line, in smaller print stated, "Negative U.N. Vote Last Night Ignored by U.S."

After the paper had passed through the hands of everyone there, and a suspended silence passed over the room, Shirley observed, "Sorry, guys, but that's the end of our investigation of Bryce. We don't have a thing on him at this point, and he'll probably be back at his old beat in New York tomorrow. Incidentally, though, his paper didn't get their story out either, did they?"

Then, apparently thinking further about the newspaper's headline, she mused out loud, "It makes you wonder though, doesn't it? Is that what we gave up all our liberties for?"

Sitting at his desk in front of his now-darkened monitor, Karl mulled over Shirley's question for a moment or two. Surprisingly, it really sounded a little like Jill's point of view. He was reminded of his first introduction to the Audio-Visual room, with its stunning lectures showing them the new, state-of-the-art method of video surveillance. Next, he reviewed in his mind the actual tapes he had seen—all seemingly of ordinary Americans in their homes, often discussing political issues in front of their TVs and ordinary day-to-day problems. Then he replayed in his mind the tape of the meeting taking place at the *Times,* and the reference to their reporter's difficulty in getting any hard information about Razik in Washington.

And that twisting scenario of events led him to a startling question of his own: *Are we really investigating foreign agents and spies here, or are we involved in spying on ordinary Americans who are trying to get information from the media and then exercise their own rights of thought and self-expression? Could this foreign counterintelligence really be designed to protect a rapidly evolving military state?*

With those somber musings, he slipped out of the room, unnoticed he thought, and headed for home. But as he went, he had to fight off an even more corrosive thought: Could Jill, in her intuitive and emotional way, actually be right after all? Perhaps about some people at the top levels. And maybe some of the designers. But he wasn't that way, and nobody that he knew was either.

XVI
Hanky Panky on the Hill

The incoming call was taken by Agent Joe Jelski, who listened closely to the unknown female voice. "Yes, we take tips and complaints here. Oh yes, we do try to accommodate people like that, and take their complaints in a discrete place. Well, that is my job—to take down information like that, and you could come to my office in the J. Edgar Hoover Building, third floor, room 307. Yes, this afternoon would be fine—in about a hour, yes. I will be looking for you. And your name is? Megan Meehan—Okay, fine."

About twenty-five minutes later, Jelski received a knock on the door of his office. His secretary led in a young woman in of about thirty-three, who appeared to be very red-faced and flustered. "You know, I really hate to do this, but I feel I have to," she blustered out as soon as she took the chair offered by Agent Jelski. "Oh, I forgot, I'm Megan. I just called you."

"Glad to meet you," Jelski rejoined, "what can we do for you?"

"Well, you know, I always was a great admirer of J. Edgar Hoover, the way he built up the FBI from nothing, and established totally new traditions. The way he would take on anyone. Not just the good guys against the bad guys, you know."

He was in the middle of a busy afternoon, so Jelski interjected. "Yes, he did a lot. Enables us to help people like you with your particular complaint—which was—what was it now?"

"Oh yes," she grimaced a bit, obviously feeling the pressure of being in the building she had heard so much about. "It's hard to know where to start. Well, I guess I should tell you who I am. I told you my name, I think, Megan. Uh, Megan Meehan. My mother would not like to hear what I have to tell you."

"Well, yes, we all have very embarrassing things happen to us that we don't like to talk about," Jelski added quietly. "And your problem is?"

"Oh, yes, well, I work on Capitol Hill for a congressman. A very well-known and respected congressman—for thirty years he's been here. The problem is that when his wife is away, back in Wyoming a lot of the time, the poor congressman is left all by himself. And, well, I am single and live by myself in Georgetown, and when his wife is out of town, or sometimes when she doesn't feel well and goes to bed early to rest up, he would call me up at my apartment at night. Well, you know, unfortunately, one thing led to another. He'd stop over for a chat, and talk about the day's problems in the office, and he often had difficult things to work out, so I would have to get him a drink, and, well, I guess you could say we're having somewhat of an affair."

"Well, that is not necessarily an infraction of the law," Jelski quickly pointed out. "It depends on state law," he added, to ease the pressure that was building. In addition, this was not necessarily the type of law enforcement that they liked to get into. The FBI wasn't family court.

Perhaps feeling that she was being taken too lightly, Megan retorted, "Well, that's really not why I'm here. I know I'm not the first woman to have an affair on Capitol

Hill. There's more to it than *that.* You see, he tells me about everything that happens. Really, if I didn't feel I had to do it to keep my job, I'm sure I wouldn't be involved with a married man. I'm Catholic, you know."

Jelski merely nodded knowingly.

"Well, anyway," she ventured somewhat more confidently, "I have no idea why a man comes in from the FBI office two or three times a week, just as we are closing for the evening."

Pointedly, Jelski queried quickly, "Why would somebody be coming into your office from here every week?"

"I have no idea," she responded, "I thought maybe it was some type of official business, and you could tell *me.* He just says to 'give this package to the Congressman.' Same thing every time. The little envelope or package is just about the same every time."

"That's odd," Jelski mused, "are you sure he's from the FBI?"

"Well, no, I'm really not. He never actually told me that, but one time I noticed that he had a identification badge on the left lapel of his shirt that said, FBI employee and it had a badge number on it."

Maybe a fake, Jelski thought, saying, "That doesn't sound like an agent's identification card. Who did he say he was?"

"Well, he said he was an old friend of the congressman—name was Ray—and that he runs errands for the congressman regularly. Sort of a runner. 'Could I just give the package or envelope to the Congressman,' he usually says. And when I mention that to the congressman, he said, 'Oh yes, Ray, that's fine. He gets things for me regularly at the store when I don't have time.' "

By this time Jelski had gotten out a yellow pad and was

writing everything down. He looked serious. Hard to tell what this was about. "Is that the whole story?" he asked.

"No, not really," she answered. "I really don't think I should be having an affair like this with a married man, but I'm afraid I'll lose my job if I call it off."

"You mentioned that earlier, I think," Jelski parried, "but is there any proof?"

"I think so," Megan responded, "because he goes out with another girl in the office too. I could ask her."

Thinking quickly, Jelski responded, "No, I don't think so. That wasn't quite what I meant. Is there anything else you want to tell us?"

"Well, something funny is going on with this corporation out in Virginia, I think." Megan added, somewhat uncertainly.

"Why is that?" asked Jelski cooperatively.

"Well, they're a big supporter of the congressman, of course. But they communicate back and forth regularly with each other, not just at election time. And every time the congressman is out of town and Ray comes in with his envelope, I'm supposed to send the envelope directly to the corporation over in Virginia."

"That is an odd coincidence, isn't it?" Jelski noted. "What is the name of the corporation?"

"The ATM Corporation," she replied without hesitation.

"Do you have any idea what is in the envelope? Have you ever opened it?"

"No, the congressman said not to bother opening it. Just place it in our interoffice memo folder, and leave it for our direct delivery service man. In fact, he once told me specifically never to open the envelope. It was a personal item, not professional.

"And then there is also that Arab businessman that

travels with the congressman, sometimes to the Middle East and sometimes to the Caribbean in the winter time," Megan seemed to add as an afterthought as if she had perhaps forgotten to mention it earlier.

"Megan, I think I have the picture here," Jelski said in an effort try to close out the interview. "I want to think about this a bit, do a little research, and talk to some other people in our office about this. I'm not sure what we will want to do on this. It is very circumstantial. Really, there is no proof of any outright crime here, and it gets right into the middle of the personal life of the congressman a good deal, without a lot of backup. But we do want to thank you for coming in, and for the kind remarks about the FBI. Thank you."

Seemingly disappointed, Megan sighed and got up slowly to leave, looking around like a tourist as she did so. "Well then, have a nice day," she said as she left. Jelski nodded and tried to smile a bit to reassure her.

When she closed the door, he immediately picked up the phone and called Silovich, "Got something here you might want to take a gander at," he said. "Can you stop by my office?"

"Be right over," barked Silovich.

When Silovich had settled in, Jelski said, "Listen to this. It just came in from an employee of a congressman we know on Capitol Hill. Thought you might want to see what you think about it." Then he started to replay the taped recording of the complaint he had just received from Megan Meehan. Silovich listened intently, with a somewhat surprised expression on his face. "Well, what do you think, just a jealous secretary prying into her boss's business to get revenge, or what?" asked Jelski. "Do we drop it, or look into it?"

Silovich was silent for quite a while and seemed to be

totally absorbed, finally saying, "Congressman Dunder is a big supporter of the Patriot Act. Always treats us well on Capitol Hill. Nobody's perfect either, you know. In some ways those congressman have very tough lives. Living alone in the pressure cooker here in Washington. But something doesn't jibe here. How could someone from the FBI be going to the congressman's office all the time? Of course, this Ray guy—or whoever he is—apparently never said he was from the FBI. Maybe he forgot, though, just that one time, he forgot to take off the badge. But he doesn't sound like an agent. Or he could be someone totally unconnected with us."

Finally, seemingly having run through all the apparent possibilities, he came to the conclusion. "Suppose he could be someone else, or he could, in fact, or in theory at least, be from this office. Maybe we'll have to check this out. I'm inclined to think so. Better call Erskine and ask him to stop over to my office in about an your. Maybe you should be there too. See you then."

XVII
The Investigation

Silovich was no procrastinator. He got himself organized in a hurry. When Erskine and Jelski arrived he had everything laid out in his mind, or so it seemed.

"Well, we've got a three-pronged problem here. First, a congressman who has been an insider on national security issues for years has made the mistake, apparently or possibly, of getting in tight with a foreign national from Saudia Arabia, even to the extent of traveling with him several times. If he actually went to the Caribbean with him, as Megan claims, that looks suspiciously like either vacation or entertainment. That's not good if he's also talking public policy with him, or public business, such as legislation or business contracts. So that gets us in under both the FISA and Patriot Act for starters. I'll give you the details on that, Joe, in a little while.

"Next, there's somebody on Capitol Hill saying that a guy from the FBI stops at the congressman's office fairly often, delivering envelopes which are supposed to go to the congressman, which the congressman says is private business of his. But then, when the congressman is away, the assistant is supposed to have them delivered over to a company in Virginia by private courier. That's not good either, if there is a shred of truth to it. And that's what we've got to find out.

"Lastly, we've got this soap-opera allegation that the

congressman is getting it on with his female employee. That's bad enough, but in addition she claims she's doing it under compulsion—if she doesn't she'll get fired. And then she claims another female in the office could probably testify to the same thing. Frankly, I really don't believe all this guff about our old friend, Congressman Frank Dunder, but I'd say we've got to check it out. But I always thought he was the solid citizen type.

"Karl, that's probably all the time you need to take on this for now. Joe, I'll give you the instructions for preparing the application to the FISA court. But could you give Megan a call back right now and ask her to give you a detailed description of this guy Ray 'whoever'—approximate age, hair and eye color, size and weight. And what type of clothes does he have on when he comes in—business suits or overalls or what? When you get that, take the description to security, and then, if necessary to personnel, and ask them if they've ever seen anybody like that around here. And is there anything else distinctive about the guy? Does he walk with a limp? Right or left handed? If she saw, any scars or facial markings, sour or friendly type, whatever. Get going on all that today—now. And find out the name of her phone company too, please.

"Now, Joe, better get out your pad and get this down. First, we want to get out an NSR—a national security letter—to Megan's phone company. We can do that on our own. We don't need any court supervision whatsoever to send that out. All we have to do is to allege that it is needed for an ongoing investigation—so make sure that you officially open a file in this case first, before you write the letters. That letter entitles us to get all the info we need on the particular account at the phone company.

"Now, as to the file on this case, put it under the name of the informant, and note on it that it is an informant file.

We're certainly not going to open a file on the congressman based on his 'hearsay' guff And even if we did, we could have a problem keeping this information secure—away from the congressman. Sometimes the walls do in fact have ears, as the saying goes.

"Now, as to the phone records, get all her—Megan's—phone records for the past six months. Too bad to intrude on all her personal stuff there, but we have to because we can't go after the congressman's records at this point. By checking the informant's records, we can check her credibility to see if she has been dreaming a lot, or if this stuff is actually true. At the same time we're checking on her credibility we can also see what we can find out about the congressman to boot."

Continuing, he then said, "We'll probably have to use 'radar' at her apartment to verify, so we'll need the make and model of the TV set, and we'll have to find out if she's got cable or satellite, and who it is.

"Next, we'll have to make an application to the FISA court, which you'll be drafting, Joe, for an order under sections 214 and 216 of the Patriot Act for ingoing and outgoing phone numbers for the next six months—that's the pen register and track and trace device orders. All we need for that is an allegation that the information is needed for a foreign intelligence investigation—and that the devices are likely to reveal information relevant to that intelligence investigation. In this case, we need this information from Megan—we'll code her as 'conduit'—to determine whether she is a credible witness generally and as to her allegation about the subject's relationship with the Arab businessman. Also, if the congressman actually comes to her place, he might make phone calls to the Arab from there—so that should do it for FISA. You can also say it would be relevant to an ongoing criminal investigation—that would be the coercive sex charge, as well as possibly something with the ATM Corporation. Of course, we don't have to have anything definite on that at this point. Before Patriot and FISA we would have to allege facts to establish it was likely a crime had been committed, but no more!

"In the FISA application we're also going to need a wiretap on Megan's residence under section 218 of the Patriot Act. She would be madder than hell if she found out—she files the complaint against the Congressman, but she gets bugged and he doesn't—but she'll never know about it because we will allege that it would have an adverse effect on our key witness and the case itself if we have to give her notice. So make the request for an indefinite delay—forever, that it is. Once again, we no longer have to say that it is likely that a crime has taken place—all we have to say is that a significant purpose of the tap is to get 'foreign intelligence information—that would be the Arab businessman element of it.

"We'll use this preliminary discovery to check the witness, see if there is a relationship with the congressman, and to see if we can pick up anything on either this Ray guy, or on the Arab guy. If we do get something concrete in the first part of this investigation, then we'll have to go back to FISA later for a 215 and 213 order—the sneak and peak entrance into her place, and also for the order for the radar. That's where you will come in on this, Karl—monitoring the radar. You will need to know what this is all about before you do your monitoring.

"The radar is likely going to be the key here, both because we could get a picture of Dunder at Megan's place and also because we could pick up on any chatter there about either Ray or the Arab, if that occurs there. If something really materializes here, we may then want to go back to the FISA court for something on the congressman himself, if we think we can keep it secret. That's it, so get tracking on this, Joe."

XVIII
Trip to the "Secret Court"

About three weeks later, with the first round of information collected and sitting in his file, Sam Silovich sat down to review the file. The request for telephone logs established one thing for a certainty—thc congressman definitely called Megan Meechan at home at night quite a bit. Since the wiretaps themselves took longer to work through the system after being approved by the FISA court, the wiretap log and tapes hadn't come yet, so he didn't know what transpired in the conversations themselves. Somewhat surprisingly, though, Megan hadn't been exaggerating as to the frequency or hours of his calls.

So the first part of Megan Meehan's allegations about Congressman Dunder were at least partly true. The next problem was to check out her other accusations, about the deliveries by the person with the FBI identification badge on, the Arab business connection with the congressman, and some connection to the ATM Corporation in Virginia. But this was going to be difficult. So far, they really had nothing illegal—a few harmless telephone calls from a congressman to an employee. Legally, that alone was worth exactly nothing. No crime. Not even a smoking gun, so to speak. Knowing an Arab was certainly not a crime, nor was traveling to the Middle East or the Caribbean.

Sam was acutely aware of the fact that before FISA and

the Patriot Act he would have had exactly nothing at this point, and he could not have gotten the permission of any judge or court to conduct any further intrusive investigation on Megan Meehan, not to speak of the congressman. No information about telephone calls, no wiretap, no search of the home. But now it was different! He could get permission from the courts to carry on a full investigation at this point. Through the FISA court he could get right into Megan's apartment legally, conduct a search, look for any tangible items of proof, find out who was talked to on the phone, put on a wiretap to see what was said on the phone, and even establish a monitoring system where he could watch what was going on inside her apartment all day long, and record each and every conversation that took place there. He had full access to her whole life—as soon as it was approved by the FISA court. That was a prosecutor's dream—and, because of those recent laws, it would all be kept totally secret from both Megan and the public, forever—and that was next!

That made it expedient to get started on a full-fledged investigation. So he called Joe and Karl to get them back into his office again. Karl would come in mainly as an observer at this point, although he probably would have some actual work to do later on the tapes.

After they had arrived and arranged themselves in the chairs in his office, he started, "Gentlemen, our next step will be a trip to the FISA court—the so-called Secret Court—again! Joe, I want you to prepare another application to the 'Star Chamber.' "

He joked about the old English court of the sixteenth century, which also had been secret, and which had been used to investigate and convict prominent and difficult persons, such as nobles—the politicians of their day—for failing to follow the leadership of King Henry VII, in order to make the point that they had the means to bring this case to a conclusion. The Star Chamber had not been bound by the rules of the common law, and neither was the FISA court bound by the rules of the common law, and neither was the FISA court bound by the rules that governed the ordinary federal courts—for instance, their records were kept secret forever—their decisions were not published in the newspaper, and FISA records were not kept in a public clerk's office. Neither were FISA decisions subject to the same rules of procedure on appeal—in fact, the FISA court decisions were not even appealed to the same courts. They were appealed to another secret appeals court. And, since the decisions of the FISA court were kept secret forever, nobody could tell whether they followed existing legal precedents or not, much in the same manner as the Star Chamber had not been bound by the common law of its day. In effect, they could make their own set of new rules, and the public would never even know that a competing court system was supplanting the old system daily. Perfect for this potentially high profile case against a congressman, involved perhaps in a sex scandal.

Continuing his instructions to Joe, he said, "What we need here is a chance to get into Megan's place and see if we can find any further corroboration of her charges. Any of the congressman's clothes, notes from him, et cetera. So I want you to prepare an application for a Section 213 and 215 of the Patriot Act search order on her place. All we need to allege is that the search is necessary as part of an investigation to protect the U.S. from clandestine intelligence activities—in this case we can point out that the Arab that travels with the congressman could be a Saudi intelligence operative. And if we put our certification on this, the judge has to approve—he has no choice in the matter under the FISA Act. Then we request the delay in notification of the entry into her home under 213 of Patriot by saying that it would have an adverse effect on the investigation if Megan were to find out about all these things—unquestionably she would no longer cooperate with us if she knew about all this. And then we also want permission to place the radar monitoring system in operation in Megan's place. So get to it! Get the paperwork done so that we can get next door to the FISA court."

A day later, Joe Jelski reappeared in Sam Silovich's office with the completed paperwork. They contacted Karl and headed to the fifth floor FISA court, which, coincidentally, was located right next to their own Audio-Visual monitoring room.

XIX

Getting Back to Jill—II & III

Karl continued to call Jill throughout the summer. Frankly, he wished he hadn't. But he could talk with her easily and they liked to chat about the areas around Richmond, and some of the same high schools that their schools had played against. He could relax with her, and could be himself, it seemed. He hadn't wanted to leave her with a bad impression of him. After all, he certainly wasn't anything like what she had made him out to be in that ugly gesture she had made.

Nevertheless, the problem didn't seem to disappear. They couldn't talk about it, because it was classified. But he had noticed her pussyfoot gingerly around the edges of the same issue on several occasions—but he still thought he had been able to prove to her that he wasn't what she apparently had thought he was, and that was why she was avoiding a direct confrontation. He had made it clear, at least, that he personally believed in personal freedom and civil liberties.

Frankly, he just felt that he was in a hole and he couldn't get out. He didn't think he could just go out into private industry and sell his government experience in order to get another job. For one thing, he couldn't even tell them what he had been doing—that it was a responsible job and he had to have a good track record to get it in the first place.

Without being able to see his experience, he might have to take a pay cut to go into the private sector. Sometimes private employers, he had heard, didn't ever really trust former government security employees. They had the same distrust that Jill seemed to have.

But he had to have somebody to talk to and do things with, so he kept going back to the watering hole. They did a lot of things together—one Saturday they walked around the Reflecting Basin, and even took a ride in the paddle boats on the Reflecting Basin. It had been a beautiful sunny day and Jill had relaxed and really seemed to enjoy it. They visited the Museum of Modern Art and walked around on another weekend. They even went back to Rehobeth Beach again.

On one occasion Jill had even invited him over to her apartment for supper after work. He had been stunned, frankly—she turned out to be a great cook. But after supper and a glass of wine, he had gotten so sleepy that he couldn't even drive home. So he had to go in and lay down for a little nap. Jill had even let him lie down on her bed for a while, and then had come in to chat with him a bit before he went to sleep. It had turned out to be very embarrassing for him, because he was so tired that he didn't wake up until late. In fact, the sky was getting light before he got back to his apartment, took his shower, changed his clothes and just made it back into work on time the next morning.

Finally he made up his mind. A change seemed to have come over him. He would have to confront her with the problem again. So, on the very next date he said, "I have something I need to discuss with you."

Affably but somewhat flippantly she said, "Well, go ahead. What is it?"

"Well, I wanted to try to explain to you my answer to the strange 'heil' sign you gave me after we went out to eat at the restaurant in northern Maryland," he said. "You know, I am still very upset about that."

"Yess, . . ." she replied, apparently being difficult.

"Well, it's like this," he started out. "The work I do *is* confidential and I can't discuss it that much. And I really don't like it that much in many respects. But there's not much I can do about it. If I tried to switch into the private sector, I couldn't tell prospective employers about it either. That would likely make them distrustful too. I would probably have to take a pay cut, and also risk angering my current government employer. They might feel I was the man who knew too much, and put the 'electric fence' on me.

"In addition, there are other reasons for staying where I am. If I moved into another field or job, I would probably end up as Mr. Insignificant, who couldn't make a difference to anyone. At least where I am, I have some authority and can perhaps make a difference when and where it counts some day. Furthermore, I really can't afford to take a pay cut now."

"Why is that?" she countered quickly.

"Well," he said slowly, "I'm going to need the money if I'm going to get married."

She seemed to laugh slightly before saying, "You . . . why, who are *you* going to marry?"

There was a very awkward, drawn-out silence before he replied firmly, "You."

Very flustered, she retorted somewhat angrily, "Well, that's nice, when did you ask me?"

Not about to back down, Karl said, "I just did!"

It probably took about thirty seconds before she sighed and slowly said, "Oh . . . Yes."

XX
The Confrontation

Not long after that, Karl was working late in his office one day late in the fall, finally finishing up a few minutes after 5 P.M., packed a briefcase with some reading to do at home, and headed out of the building to his car. Just before reaching the Pennsylvania Avenue exit from the building, he realized that he had forgotten to pick up a pamphlet on the Patriot Act that he planned to review that evening. So he turned around and headed back up to his office. As he got off the elevator, he took a right toward the suite of offices housing the Counter-Intelligence Section, where his desk was located.

Going through the outer door of that Section, he passed a number of other offices on the way to his own. As he went by Sam Silovich's office, he noticed as he went by that there was somebody still there. Thinking to ask Sam one additional question about the Meehan file, he went back a few steps and put his head around the corner of the door. A man was working at the computer all right with his head down and looking at something on the monitor . . . but it was not Sam Silovich!

"Oh, sorry, I thought you were Sam Silovich!" he said quickly. The man at the computer looked startled. Then he quickly grabbed something out of the computer, flicked the switch on the power station, stood up, and started using a cloth sitting on the desk. As he did so he said, "Oh, that's all right, I was just cleaning up the power train on the computer." The man was about six feet tall perhaps, maybe fifty-seven years old or thereabouts, and seemed to have on the clothes of a custodial person.

Karl was a bit surprised as he listened, because the man didn't seem to have been doing any cleaning until after Karl poked his head around the corner. And would a custodial person, which was apparently what he was because of the typewritten I.D. badge on his shirt, actually be the person to clean the mainframe of the computer? He didn't think so. "What did you say your name was?"

The man obviously did not like that question. He seemed to wince as heard it. "Well, listen, no need to get in huff. I'm just the regular janitor. I've been on this shift for thirty years. Everybody knows me—you must be new here. When did you arrive?"

Irritated at the response from the janitor, Karl replied, "I've been here a couple of months. But I'm a G-12, and I've been with the government for over ten years." Bothered too by the janitor's effort to change the direction of the conversation, he did not offer his name, saying instead, "What did you say your name is?"

"Just call me Ray, everybody else does," the janitor replied, picking up his broom and cloth and heading for the door.

"Just a minute," Karl interrupted, stepping in front of the door to stop his progress. "I want to see what you took out of the computer and put in your pocket when I looked in here," he said, looking the janitor right in the eye to see how he reacted.

The janitor once again shot a darting look of anger at Karl, saying, "I've got every right to be here. I've been coming in this section, and this office, for twenty-seven years. I clean this place at night about three or four times a week," he said, obviously hoping that would get him off the hook with Karl.

But his righteous answer made Karl even more suspicious and worried, so he said, "You probably *do* have the right to be here, but you don't have any right to be in that computer." He was guessing, but it was an educated guess because he knew that all the computers in the building were cleaned and maintained by a separate office he usually called about twice a year himself when he had a computer problem. "That computer is filled with secret, intelligence information, and you must know that if you've been here that long. Don't you read the signs around here?"

That really seemed to shake up the janitor, who seemed to be reaching his wit's end. He was steaming. "Actually, I am authorized to go into that computer. In fact, I've been instructed to do it. I take out information and deliver it to another branch of government for their use."

"You've got to be kidding me," Karl retorted. "Let me see your full identification card. Are you a janitor or an agent here?" As the janitor was taking his I.D. card out of his wallet, Karl added, "And I want to see a written authorization to go into that computer, or I'm reporting this to Sam Silovich. Who told you to go into that computer? Are you authorized to go into any computer around here? Are you out of your mind going into a computer in the Counter-Intelligence Section? Don't you know that's against the law?"

At that point, Sam Silovich, who was also working late, walked back into the office—his office, saying, "What is going on here? Is this a tea party or what?"

Karl explained quickly, "I saw somebody in here as I went by, thought it was you, and came in to ask you a question. Instead, this guy was here, and was working on your computer. As I came in, he took something out of it and put it in his pocket. When I asked to see what it was, he said he was the regular janitor here and claimed he had the right to go into your computer. But he won't show me what he took out of it. Says he is authorized to take out information and deliver it to another branch of government."

Silovich looked as though he was about to explode. "All right, who the hell told you you could take classified information out of my computer? And who do you deliver it to? What branch of government do you deliver it to?"

Turning red as a beet, the janitor said, "I'm authorized to deliver it to the congressional branch, for their review."

"Who the hell told you that?" Silovich demanded. "That sounds like a crock to me. Do you have that in writing?"

"Well, in a way I do. Congressman Dunder instructed me to do this for him." Apparently as proof, he pulled a typewritten piece of paper out of his wallet. "The congressman typed this out for me," he said as he handed the paper to Silovich.

"What the hell is this?" Silovich stormed, as he started to read the material written on the paper, "A person is guilty of an offense if he intentionally discloses or uses information obtained under color of law by electronic surveillance, knowing . . . that it was not authorized by statute."

"That is section 1809 of the FISA," the janitor responded quickly. "The congressman gave it to me to explain. He said if the original surveillance was authorized, and you guys only do what is authorized, that there was no prohibition against him having me access information in there," pointing to the computer. "Not only that, he said he ought to know what the statute says, and what it means, because he himself wrote the statute himself thirty years ago before it was passed by Congress!"

Just as Silovich let out a roar, "What, you've got to be kidding me!" Roger Kaiser turned the corner and walked into the room, demanding to know what the commotion was all about.

Hearing part of the janitor's argument, and Silovich's outraged response, Kaiser said, "Is this all about the criminal prohibitions in the FISA Act, section 1809, I think?"

"That's it," explained Silovich. "He says some congressman authorized him to go into these files, and take out information and deliver it to Capitol Hill for their use."

"I don't know what congressman said what," Kaiser rejoined, "but my understanding is that he is correct about the meaning of the statute. In fact, it is a defense, if I am not mistaken, to any criminal charge of misuse of information that the 'surveillance was authorized by . . . a court of competent jurisdiction,' " he said, picking up a copy of the statute from Silovich's desk, and quickly opening to the section and reading from it. "That is, and has been, my understanding for some time. The statute as written doesn't deal with what is done with the information after it is lawfully collected in the first place. It only deals with the issue of *whether* it was lawfully collected in the first place. If it was, then it is lawful to use the information any way you want after that. As to what happened later, there are no prohibitions if it was lawfully collected in the first instance. That was just plain left out of the law when it was written and passed."

Given some time to think, instead of constantly talking, as he had been before Kaiser's entrance, Silovich was now rapidly putting everything together. "So you must be the mysterious Mr. X. 'Ray,' I believe the name was, is that right?" he said pointedly to the janitor.

"How did you know?" the janitor said, "you hadn't gotten here when I told this guy that," he said, pointing at Karl.

Now more reserved and controlled, and seeing the opposition he was getting from Roger Kaiser, Silovich, the attorney and senior man in the group, terminated the discussion, "Well, I'm going to get to the bottom of this. We are already investigating this matter. And I want you to stay out of all these computers until I tell you. Otherwise, I'm going to have your job, Mr. Ray! And that is for sure!" With that, the group, already late in getting home, broke up for the evening.

As Karl departed the building, he could not help but think that if he had not been there, and had not gone back to pick up the memorandum, the whole issue might not have come up in the first place.

And, as Sam Silovich left, he kept thinking, knowing what he already knew from what Megan Meehan had already reported, that the real question here might not be resolved just by the one statutory clause alone. There could be other things involved in this case. Certainly, they already seemed to have inadvertently corroborated a good part of Meehan's story themselves. What about the rest of it?

XXI

The Arm of Justice Strikes

Silovich wasted no time after getting to the office the next day. He went right to work on the Meehan—now re-named by him the "conduit" file—case immediately. He had enough now to get back into the FISA court with an application for a section 213 and 215 order, to search the premises—not of Megan Meehan—now it was the premises of the residence of Ray the janitor—Ray Barnes it had turned out to be—their own FBI and Justice Building janitor of thirty years' standing.

And he was startled when the employment office gave him the information on where Ray Barnes lived—in plush Farquahr County, Virginia—on a 125-acre beef farm. And the county assessment records indicated that the farm was operational and usually had one-hundred head of prize Hereford beef cattle on it. Incredibly, it was assessed for over $1,500,000. And this guy was a janitor?

Several weeks later, after obtaining the order from the FISA court to search the Barnes farm, and actually having the search completed by the FBI, Silovich had some documents in hand that were really interesting to him. The search party had found an office in the barn where the cattle were housed in bad weather. The office had all the operating records in it for the beef cattle business that was obviously being conducted there.

The records indicated that each Hereford was currently being sold at cattle auctions outside of Richmond for about $2,500. And there were, in fact, currently about 120 head of cattle on the farm, all properly registered to Ray Barnes, and all having been properly registered by the National Hereford Association of America as purebreds. *So the cattle alone were worth about $300,000,* concluded Silovich. So that left the question of where the cattle had come from.

And the thorough search had come up with an answer to that also. There were bills of lading and receipts discovered by the investigators. The invoices showed the date of delivery for each Hereford on the premises. They also showed the name of the party to which they were delivered—Ray Barnes, the date and location of the delivery, and the name of the farm making the delivery, a "Prince farm" in southern New York State. In fact, they were perfectly ordinary delivery papers, except for one thing—they neglected to provide a receipt for the amount paid for each Hereford delivered. No purchase price was included anywhere.

One other thing was notable about the delivery paperwork. Each piece of paper contained a reference to a third party, each stating in the lower lefthand corner—"cc. ATM Corporation, Sampson, Virginia." Sam Silovich knew what that meant immediately. Next stop, a sneak and peek warrant for the premises of the ATM Corporation in suburban Virginia!

After that, the investigation rolled forward for another five months. The U.S. attorney for the Northern District of Virginia was brought into the case, and worked under Silovich's direction. Several other people from the office of Congressman Dunder, including his legislative assistant

Jake Reinwater and the congressman himself, were also interviewed and then investigated very thoroughly.

They also talked to a very nervous Megan Meehan several more times to straighten out some details in the case. About three months after that, an article appeared in most of the local papers. Since the articles were all almost identical it appeared to be a Justice Department release. The headline read:

> FBI JANITOR AND CONGRESSMAN ACCOMPLICE INDICTED IN 'INFORMATION FOR SALE' DEAL. Congressional aide to congressman cops plea and agrees to testify against boss. Janitor caught red-handed with hand in cookie jar of counter-Intelligence information. Janitor had farm in Farquahr County, Virginia with 150 acres and 120 head of prize cattle—Indictment alleges ATM Corporation was middleman, delivering free cattle to janitor in return for information.

The article itself read:

> The U.S. Attorney for northern Virginia announced a 62-count indictment today against Congressman Dunder from Wyoming, an FBI janitor, and the ATM Corporation, for stealing top secret counter-intelligence information. In an unusual scheme, the indictment alleges that a thirty-year FBI janitor-employee was caught red-handed by an FBI agent on a Saturday afternoon stealing information off the computer of a counter-intelligence operative. The indictment alleges that the employee had been stealing intelligence information off the computers in a secret counter-intelligence office in the Justice Department for approximately 20 years.
>
> The disks of information taken off the computer were taken by the janitor after work to the office of Congressman Dunder periodically—sometimes almost daily—where

they were then delivered to the ATM Corporation in northern Virginia, to be used for an undisclosed purpose.

The indictment further alleges that the janitor then received payment in the form of prize beef cattle which were delivered by the ATM Corporation to the janitor's farm, free of charge. The farm and cattle are now worth approximately $1,800,000, according to the indictment.

The indictment alleges that the congressman's aide then solicited and received large political contributions from the ATM Corporation, in consideration of the information received by them from the Congressman's office. The aide has agreed to testify against his former boss.

Ironically, the congressman had been one of the original draftsman and sponsors of both the FISA and Patriot counter-intelligence acts, the very same acts pursuant to which the information stolen had been gathered in the first place.

END